Josh was proving every bit as tempting as she'd imagined

He stood close, one hand on either side of Lexi, bracketing her against the door. The dominant position made her think about lying beneath him in her bed, his arms levering him above her body as he made love to her.

At that moment she looked up at him, only to find his gaze focused on her mouth.

He made a hungry sound that rumbled right through her in the moment before his mouth met hers. She shivered at the wet heat of the kiss, and twisted her way closer to the hard wall of his chest.

Josh's hands moved to hold her against him. He stroked his way down her spine, sealing her body to his. His arousal nudged her belly, making her want to drag him inside and indulge herself in him.

Suddenly he pried himself away.

"Honey, I need to know if this is what you want."

Lexi wriggled against him shamelessly, wanting more of this feeling. "Don't make me break out the handcuffs again, Detective. You're not going anywhere tonight."

Dear Reader,

New York police detective Josh Winger has never been so relentlessly pursued, but then again, he's never had fashion critic Lexi Mansfield on his tail before. He needs to remain anonymous to protect his drug-smuggling investigation, yet Lexi seems determined to drag him into the spotlight. When the outrageous beauty clicks a pair of handcuffs on him at a ritzy buy-a-celebrity's-freedom fund-raiser, Josh doesn't know whether to put up a fight...or encourage her.

I had so much fun writing Lexi and Josh's story. These characters first appeared in my Blaze novel #26, *Silk, Lace & Videotape* last February, and they captured my imagination from the moment they stepped on the scene. I hope you enjoy their rocky—and very steamy—road to love.

Visit me at www.JoanneRock.com to learn more about future releases or to let me know what you think of Lexi and Josh. I'd love to hear from you!

Happy reading!

Joanne Rock

P.S. Don't forget to check out tryblaze.com!

Books by Joanne Rock

HARLEQUIN BLAZE
26—SILK, LACE & VIDEOTAPE

HARLEQUIN TEMPTATION
863—LEARNING CURVES

IN HOT PURSUIT

Joanne Rock

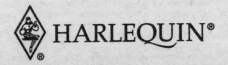

TORONTO • NEW YORK • LONDON
AMSTERDAM • PARIS • SYDNEY • HAMBURG
STOCKHOLM • ATHENS • TOKYO • MILAN • MADRID
PRAGUE • WARSAW • BUDAPEST • AUCKLAND

To my father and favorite storyteller, Cornelius Goes.
If I can weave a tale half as entertaining as the ones you've
been telling me all my life, I count myself fortunate indeed.
To my mother, Louise, thank you for the unwavering support
and for showing me how to move through life
with quiet strength and grace.

I am grateful to you both for the model of
your marriage——a wonderful testament
to happily-ever-afters.

ISBN 0-373-79052-X

IN HOT PURSUIT

Copyright © 2002 by Joanne Rock.

Visit us at www.eHarlequin.com

Printed in U.S.A.

1

"STEP ASIDE, LADIES. Jailer coming through." Dangling handcuffs from her manicured fingers, Lexi Mansfield swept past the other socialites thronging the ladies' room mirror in the trendy Manhattan bar.

She didn't need to see her reflection to confirm she looked as good as her hodgepodge of features would allow. She'd blown two paychecks to ensure New York's best hair and makeup people maximized her questionable beauty assets for tonight's fund-raiser.

A girl couldn't go into battle unarmed, after all.

She stuffed her handcuffs into her purse for safe-keeping until her jailer stint for tonight's Buy a Celebrity's Freedom event kicked in. She would have served as MC tonight, if not for the rampant gossip currently making the rounds about her. Being demoted to jailer might be a step down, but Lexi was determined to wrest all the fun she could out of the handcuffs.

Behind her, a compact snapped close and a pair of high heels clicked double time on the ceramic tile. "Hold up, Lex," Lexi's girlfriend Amanda called.

Lexi forced herself to stop, even though she couldn't wait to leave the smothered giggles and gossipy whispers of the powder room behind. She knew all too well that *she* was the hot topic of the night, and the knowledge ate away at her stomach far more than did the two glasses of merlot—although the smoke and hair spray fumes didn't help much, either.

No doubt the ladies' room rumor mill couldn't wait for Lexi to scram so they could continue their discussion of the day's scandal. Lexi Mansfield—one of New York's leading fashion reviewers and most popular magazine columnists—had been shredded to ribbons in a scathing letter to the editor written by an up-and-coming designer.

The designer in question, Simone Bertrand, had been Lexi's nemesis since boarding school. A trust-fund baby with more boobs than brains, Simone had the morals of a tomcat, but her scads of money usually covered up the fact.

Amanda smoothed a hand over a nonexistent stray lock of light brown hair and frowned at Lexi. "You are dangerous tonight. I about twisted my heel to catch up with you."

Lexi couldn't help a twinge of envy for her gorgeous friend, a ringer for a young Grace Kelly, except for the darker hair. Despite Lexi's designer duds and expensive makeup job, she paled in comparison to Amanda's born beauty.

"Amanda, I appreciate what you're doing, but you don't need to baby-sit me. I'm a big girl, I can handle the gossip hounds." Lexi opened the bathroom door to greet the pulsing bass of a pop dance tune.

Amanda pushed the door shut again and grabbed Lexi by the elbow. Lexi squealed, but allowed her friend to tug her back into the restroom toward the semi-quiet corner by a condom-dispensing machine.

Lexi snorted at the picture of the ecstatic-looking couple plastered on the front of the dispenser. It had been far too long since Lexi had needed condoms for a damn thing.

"Why do I get the feeling you *want* me to leave?" Amanda huffed, crossing her arms over her blue taffeta gown. "Don't tell me you'd rather face the vultures by yourself."

Lexi shrugged. "Maybe I'd be better off facing them on my own, so people can say what they want about the letter and get it over with." The charity they were raising money for tonight—Shelter the Homeless—was one of Lexi's pet projects. She wouldn't leave until she'd done her job.

Amanda studied her for a moment. "Are you sure?"

What was the worst people could say? *I agree with Simone's letter to the editor and I think you are a blot on the concept of style, too? I second Simone's observation that you have all the magnetism of a houseplant?* Besides, Simone's public attack might be embarrassing, but it didn't scare Lexi half as much as the anonymous threatening notes she had been receiving for the past month.

She didn't breathe a word of those letters to anyone, however. Lexi had grown accustomed to fending for herself a long time ago.

Lexi nodded. "I'm sure. I've made my entrance. I've scoped out my territory. I'm ready to take them on."

"I don't know, Lex." Amanda glanced uncertainly over one shoulder toward the crowd of cackling social divas spritzing hair spray and layering on lipstick. "They look like they can't wait to get their talons into you. Want me to wait until the Buy a Celebrity's Freedom event begins? Once you start your gig locking up the celebs, you should be okay."

Lexi still fumed to think she would be stuck filling the makeshift jail cell with wealthy patrons. She should be the MC tonight, but after the scathing letter, the charity had asked her to let someone else take center stage.

"If they get too rough before then, I'll just latch on to someone else." Lexi eyed the stud on the condom machine and wondered if maybe tonight she'd live on the wild side and find herself another protector—one who wore a tux instead of blue taffeta. "Besides, how can I feel like I have more magnetism than a houseplant when I'm walking around next to the Revlon girl?" She shoved Amanda toward the door. "Get lost, girlfriend. You've got better ways to spend your Saturday night."

Amanda flashed a wicked grin. "Duke *did* say something about waiting up for me."

"See?" Lexi brushed away an escapee spiral of hair from her face and winked. "You're supposed to be packing for your getaway, anyway. What time do you leave tomorrow?"

"Nine. I can't believe he's taking me on a motorcycle trip. I've never done anything so exciting in my whole life."

"Call me a city girl, but I don't know if three days

perched on a motorcycle seat is my idea of fun." Lexi grinned, the first smile she'd managed since waking to find the derisive letter to the editor in the very magazine she'd given the past five years of her life to. "Go home, Amanda. I can take it from here."

Amanda nodded as she adjusted Lexi's borrowed diamond collar. "You're right. You look ready to kick some gossipmonger hind-end."

Lexi laughed, tugging open the rest room door. "I dressed to kill for a reason, honey." She withdrew her silver handcuffs from her purse and slid one end over her wrist. "Besides, maybe I can squeeze a small amount of satisfaction from my detractors by playing the dominatrix."

"No brutality, Lex," Amanda warned. "And if you find yourself in any provocative situations with those cuffs, I highly recommend capturing it on videotape."

Lexi laughed, knowing she'd never have anywhere near the kind of sizzling adventures Amanda had stumbled into a few months ago with Duke Rawlins.

"I'll leave the video to you. I'm just going to have fun being Lexi, Mistress of the Night."

After they exchanged a quick hug near the bar, however, Lexi's smile faded as she watched Amanda disappear in the cloakroom.

Leaving Lexi alone to fend for herself.

In a room stuffed full of people who couldn't wait to see her crumble.

Lexi clutched the polished mahogany bar and took deep breaths to ward off the feeling she'd just made a colossal mistake by excusing her bodyguard. The fashion world elite adored Amanda, the socially untouchable daughter of one of New York's most influential designers. Lexi was a scrapper, a New Jersey transplant to Long Island's upper-crust North Shore and eventually Manhattan's fashion world. Although devoid of blue blood, she possessed a sharp eye and wit for commenting on style. And tonight, she was fair game for this crowd.

Lexi was thankful that Simone Bertrand had not attended this function. But then, Simone resented spending a cent on anyone but herself. Lexi knew the author of the *other* letters could be here tonight, however, and the thought gave her pause.

The notes had urged her to change topics in her column—or she'd be sorry. But Lexi often covered three or four different topics each week, and she could never be sure which topic in particular the note-writer referenced.

Not that it would have shut Lexi up.

Her need to speak her mind was as essential as breathing. She'd been hushed far too many times as a child. She didn't let anybody muzzle her these days.

As the band switched from a pop disco beat to a swing set, Lexi struggled to gather her bearings. Peering around the two-tiered disco that had closed its doors to the public for the fund-raiser, Lexi spied no friendly faces in the crowd. The elegant sea of tuxes and silk seemed to have closed ranks against her. She hadn't felt like such an outsider since childhood, peeking into her parents' book-lined study and wishing she could be a part of their academic discussions.

Ignoring the urge to bolt and return to the security

of her apartment full of nonjudgmental pets, Lexi reminded herself she was here for a good cause. The Shelter the Homeless organization had always been dear to her heart, and she ran frequent reminders of their activities as footnotes in her fashion column.

Bracing herself for a night of mingling with the masses and imprisoning anyone she thought might bring in a big donation, Lexi approached the small platform and podium to immerse herself in her duties. She could inspect the makeshift jail cell—sort of a sixties-style go-go booth—that would house her captives. This would be more fun than an auction. Lexi merely had to handcuff celebrities and toss them in the cell, while the MC coerced the crowd into making a donation to free the jailbird.

The jailer job was a definite step down from hosting the event, but she'd be damned if she would walk out of here tonight before last call. At least everyone would see her on stage, head held high, rather than cowering in the corner sucking down Fuzzy Navels.

Determined to parlay her frustration into her role as the bad girl cop, Lexi sauntered off into the crowd in search of her first victim.

AN HOUR LATER, Lexi realized she was not only far removed from her dominatrix fantasy, but also was enduring far more snide remarks than she'd ever anticipated.

In the course of rounding up various fashion industry stars, she'd heard several versions of "here comes the houseplant," two backhanded comments that she looked lovely in her "usual, nonmagnetic style,'' and one outright slam that she had finally received her comeuppance for playing goddess of the fashion world.

Lexi retreated to the bar and ordered a cosmopolitan—pretty much a martini, but the pink color made it look innocent. Wavering between tears and fury, she swayed to the Latin beats the band had switched to, trying not to glance at her watch. She didn't want to know how many more hours she had to endure the lions' den.

Public humiliation she could deal with. But did her social circle really view her as the most unattractive woman in Manhattan? Sure, they veiled their insults by attacking her fashion stance. But the whispers she'd heard all night had been directed at her—her gaudy look, her tacky clothes, her attempts to fit into a world that didn't seem to have room for her.

Lexi peered down at her sequined dress, knowing it epitomized refinement. Could she help it that her tiny frame didn't fill it out the way Amanda's would? Was it such a crime that she didn't care to butcher her Romanesque nose with a surgeon's knife so she could meet some prepackaged, Stepford ideal of beauty?

Maybe she could feel a little more self-righteous about her sense of style and personal magnetism if she'd actually attracted a man in the past few years. She'd told herself she had no love life because she dedicated her time to her job. What if lack of time had nothing to do with it? What if she couldn't lure a man to her bed for all the lingerie in the Victoria's Secret catalog?

The notion scared her to her *peau de soie* covered toes.

An image of the stud on the condom dispenser flashed in her mind. What if she went in search of a man here, tonight?

She glanced around the disco at the guys in perfect tuxes, the ones who didn't dance too much so as not to mess up their hair. How could she ever find a man among the Ken look-alike dolls who—

Her gaze stopped abruptly on a slightly rumpled dinner jacket at the back of the room. Her eyes followed the dark fabric upward to glimpse a white shirt and a long tie—not a standard bow tie—that wavered between gray and silver.

A waiter passed in front of the man, a tray of drinks hiding the stranger's face from view. Lexi set her drink aside and leaned forward to get a better look. As the tray passed, she spied a profile to set a girl's pulse to racing.

Dark hair brushed his collar, too short to be a rock star's hair, but definitely longer than the cropped perfection of every other man in the room. Great cheekbones. A nose that definitely hadn't bowed down to the gods of plastic surgery. And a diamond stud earring winking in one lobe.

Hello.

Blood pulsed through her veins in time with the sultry Latin rhythm that dominated the disco. Maybe the stress of the day conspired to make her a little more on edge tonight, but she'd never before experienced lust quite so keenly just looking at a man.

An idea took shape in her head—a crazy, insane

plan to act on this feeling. Lexi slid off her bar stool before she lost her nerve to approach the sexy stranger.

She downed half the cosmopolitan to fuel her steps in the direction of her quarry. The pair of handcuffs around her wrist would provide a definite conversational icebreaker.

Lexi had just figured out a surefire way to put her personal magnetism to the test.

JOSH WINGER didn't need to look over his shoulder to know someone followed him. After all, he'd been chased by the best—bad asses with guns, knives and garrotes for weapons rather than six-inch spikes and a killer flash of thigh.

The sultry brunette in black sequins had stalked him through the trendy Manhattan bar for the past ten minutes. Relentlessly, she pursued him—through a narrow, zebra-printed corridor, down a staircase lit in pink neon.

Damn.

Any other day, Josh would have welcomed attention from a knockout like the one hot on his trail. Tonight, however, he needed to remain detached, anonymous. He'd attended the after-hours gathering of New York's fashion elite for work, not pleasure.

Josh didn't waste any time at the subterranean bar. As soon as he hit the lower level, he sprinted along the side of the room to a second set of stairs and bolted back up them to the main floor. With any luck, the sequined siren would get distracted downstairs, and Josh would be able to get back to business.

The thought of work didn't interest him quite as much as it usually did, however. Maybe because he'd caught the brunette's eye earlier, and the look she'd shot him still sizzled through his veins. Despite the woman's designer dress and perfect makeup, Josh had the feeling she was the kind of woman who could heat up a room with nothing more than a breathy whisper....

Not that he was thinking along those lines on the job.

He needed to keep his professional ear to the ground tonight and observe the players in the fashion world. For two months, he and his partner had been tracking smuggling activity in the Garment District to no avail. But tonight, he'd slipped past the doorman at a swanky fund-raiser attended by most of the smuggling suspects on Josh's list.

One way or another, he would bring down the thugs causing trouble in the Garment District. Not only were the bastards slipping drugs and weapons into the city, but they were using underage gangsters to run half their dirty business. Josh had already tangled with one juvenile offender last month in an encounter that had nearly cost a fellow officer's life. While Josh had wasted time trying to talk the kid out of his crime, the wayward teen got off a shot that seriously injured Josh's backup. Josh blamed himself for the shooting—and so did the press when the story was splashed all over the front page.

Now Josh hungered to find the ringleader of the smuggling operation, to squash the wave of crime that had plagued his precinct and the special task force he was assigned to. If that meant working on his case after-hours, Josh didn't mind a bit. This job meant everything to him.

He scanned the crowd one more time, searching for any familiar faces.

His partner's new socialite fiancée had told Josh about the event. He'd searched for Amanda Matthews—soon-to-be Rawlins—in the crowd, but she'd obviously left before he arrived. On the other hand, maybe his partner, Duke, hadn't allowed his gorgeous future bride to stray as far as six blocks from their brownstone. The two of them seemed to be joined at the hip—a condition Josh had no intention of ever suffering.

Josh surveyed the dance floor from an old balcony left over from the bar's days as a theater. Later, the seats would be packed with couples too drunk to find a hotel room, but for now the shadowy corner gave him a perfect window on the glittering assembly below.

For a moment, he caught himself wishing he'd glimpse black sequins. He had to admit that the attention from the brunette had been more than a little flattering. He'd never been the kind of man women sought out first, which probably had something to do with the fact that he resembled a criminal more than he did a cop.

A waitress, in thigh-high boots and a dress that looked like an X-rated toga, sidled over, effortlessly balancing a tray of empty glasses with one hand. The getup might have turned his head if he hadn't just

spotted a small jail cell off to one side of the dance
floor.

A jail cell?

"Get you a drink?" the waitress asked, leaning
close to be heard over the steady thrum of the music's
bass line.

He shook his head and tore his gaze from the lower
level long enough to smile at her. "No drink, but
maybe you can tell me what the cage is for." He
peeled a crisp bill off the roll in his pocket and stuffed
it in the waitress's tip glass.

She shrugged, the small action shifting her tiny
toga enough to flash him white satin panties. An observation he made on a strictly professional basis. He
was more in the mood for black sequins, anyhow.

The blonde waitress adjusted her tray. "Some prop
for the private party. It doesn't belong to the club."
She sent him a wicked grin. "Looks sort of kinky,
huh?"

Images of the brunette in a cage didn't do much
for him, until he mentally inserted himself inside the
cage along with her.

"Definitely." He turned back to the view on the
dance floor, just in time to make eye contact with his
pursuer.

Even from this distance, her dark eyes broadcast a
message for him alone. A smile played at her crimson
lips, as if she enjoyed their game.

Heat surged through him. He admired her persis-
tence. An odd sense of pride in her tracking abilities
mixed with growing frustration. He couldn't very well
do his job tonight if he had to keep eluding this

woman. Maybe he needed to confront her and tell her he wasn't interested in her game.

Too bad his body was *very* interested.

Josh had the sinking feeling that if he got within five feet of the fashion princess, he'd be lured in like a damn fish.

Reluctantly, he left his observation deck before his stalker caught up with him. He wasn't a cop worth his badge if he couldn't give a society babe the slip, right? She was probably drunk to boot, given that she had chosen to pursue him over the wealth of high-brow guys milling around the bar tonight.

Josh sped back down the pink neon stairs and ducked into the hallway by the phone booths and cloakroom. As soon as he shook the woman on his tail, he would seat himself at the bar and salvage what he could of the night by soaking in the party gossip.

For now, he envisioned his pursuer climbing the stairs in her slinky black gown, and he ticked off enough time for her to reach the balcony he'd just vacated. Thinking she must be safely on the opposite side of the bar by now, Josh stepped from the dark hallway.

And nearly collided with a whirlwind of black sequins.

He obviously hadn't given his pursuer enough credit, because there she stood with a satisfied gleam in her dark eyes.

Her black hair shimmered in the low light of the bar. Although most of it rested on her head in an intricate knot, one long wayward tendril slipped free to point a path toward her cleavage. Cleavage outlined by a square neckline that exposed just enough pale skin to tease the hell out of him. The collar of diamonds around her throat was too sexy to even contemplate in a public place.

He instantly shifted his gaze to her face.

She arched a brow and smiled up at him. Even with her high heels, she barely reached his chin. "Excuse me. Guess I wasn't watching where I was going."

Her knowing look belied her innocent words.

He couldn't help but smile back at her. She practically preened over her small victory.

"Seems to me you were right on target."

She shrugged a careless shoulder and waved an airy hand, gestures that loosely conveyed consent to his words. Josh wondered if she always spoke so eloquently with her body. Her sequins danced and winked, giving her the illusion of perpetual motion.

"Maybe you're right," she admitted, treating him to an obvious once-over. "I just hope the reward proves to be as much fun as the chase."

Name the place, honey. The temperature between them soared a few more degrees.

The woman was a firecracker.

Josh's smuggling investigation faded into the background for one perilous moment. His work suddenly seemed as distant as the zebra-printed walls and the pulsing Latin music. This tiny woman had a bigger presence than salsa or smugglers.

But Josh wouldn't allow himself to lose focus.

Before he could respond, the woman offered a cheeky grin and a formal handshake.

"I'm Lexi Mansfield."

Josh suspected it would be dangerous to touch her, but how could he ignore such an innocuous overture? Hesitating only briefly, he closed his fingers around Lexi's long, jeweled fingers.

"Josh Winger, at your service."

She squeezed his hand back, her grip surprisingly strong for such a little thing.

"I certainly hope so, Mr. Winger."

Distracted by the wicked twinkle in her brown eyes and the exotic scent of her, Josh didn't notice the handcuffs until cold metal clamped around his wrist.

With a deft *click* of the mechanism worthy of a veteran vice detective, Josh's stalker chained herself to him.

So much for his skills as an undercover cop.

He was about to be brought low by a kinky dominatrix with killer cleavage and a lethal attitude. Lexi Mansfield had just blown his cover—and fueled all his fantasies—by handcuffing him into a naughty scenario guaranteed to attract attention.

2

LEXI'S SENSE OF ADVENTURE fled when Josh stared back at her with hard, cold eyes.

"What the hell are you doing?" He jerked the handcuffs enough to pull her forward slightly.

Luckily, her sense of indignation helped her stand her ground. "No rough stuff, mister." She held up her end of the handcuffs and jangled the links between them. "I'm at the other end of these, remember."

He looked like she'd just sentenced him to twenty-to-life. What was the big deal? She'd hauled at least ten other people to the jail cell tonight, and nobody else had caused such a fuss. If anything, they'd been more interested in giving Lexi the cold shoulder than worrying about their jail time.

Josh Winger angled his big body between her and the dance floor, shielding their conversation from any wayward eyes. "What I want to know is why I'm on this end." He hissed the words between clenched teeth. "You got some kind of fetish?"

Lexi blinked up at him, realizing the man seemed to have no clue what fund-raiser he'd bought a ticket for tonight.

"No, Mr. Winger, I don't. I happen to be the jail

mistress for the Buy a Celebrity's Freedom event tonight. Care to come with me quietly?''

He stared at her for an interminable moment, weighing her words and sizing up her person. Lexi resisted the urge to stand up straighter. She'd followed this man because she wanted to meet him, maybe lure him into a one-night stand to somehow soothe her stinging self-esteem.

Now, she realized she'd obviously forgotten how to flirt. Josh Winger remained oblivious to all her best provocation.

Finally, his gaze returned to hers, his gray eyes seeing too deeply inside her. "I can't guarantee I'll come with you quietly, Lexi—'' Was it her imagination, or did the phrase take on new meaning when it fell from his lips? "I think it depends on just how far you want to go.''

A wave of heat took a slow ride over her flesh, awakening every last nerve ending to the draw of the stud sporting one earring. His words melted the backbone she'd fought hard for all night, leaving her swaying on her high heels, and suddenly more than a little wary.

"Um.'' She fought her way out of the sensual fog to concentrate on her answer. Forget flirting. This man could out-flirt her with his hands—well, handcuffed. She'd be lucky to deposit him in the jail cell without spontaneously combusting first. "I just need to put you in the cell over there.''

She pointed toward the edge of the dance floor— anything to distract him so she could pull herself together. Maybe she'd think more clearly when they weren't handcuffed. Then she could decide whether she wanted to proceed with her plan to test out her personal magnetism.

Josh's gaze didn't follow her finger. Instead, he kept his focus directly on her.

Her sequins tread dangerously close to his dinner jacket with each breath she took. The heat of his body penetrated her lightweight gown, giving her the sense they'd already touched somehow.

What would it be like to spend a night with a man like this? Would she dare?

"Do you know who I am, Lexi?"

Too sexy for his own good?

"No."

"I'm a police detective. Tenth precinct. It's usually me who locks the people behind bars, so you caught me a little off guard here tonight."

She nodded, trying to make sense of his words. "I'm sure many of tonight's partygoers will vie to spring you from captivity, Detective. You won't have to sit behind bars for very long." Lexi had no doubt this man would start a catfight as women lined up to ransom him. She'd told herself that had been a small facet of her reason for pursuing him.

He shook his head, causing a lock of hair to fall forward on his forehead, making her hand itch to smooth it.

"You don't understand. I'm not going into the jail cell."

Lexi straightened. "You have to. Party rules."

She saw a flash of frustration in his eyes, followed by something hotter and more complex.

He reached for her with his free hand, his fingers settling on the bare skin of her arm. His touch was light but scorching, trailing down her shoulder to pause a hair's breadth from her breast.

Lexi didn't breath for fear she'd close the gap.

He leaned fractionally closer. "I'm a cop, you know. I have some experience with these." He jangled the handcuffs that bound them together.

The image *that* brought to mind was definitely X-rated. Surely she misunderstood. "Are you saying you know how to escape?"

He blinked slowly, a smile twitching his lips. "Is that what you think I'm saying?"

She had to take a breath or else she'd start hyperventilating. She gulped in smoke-filled air, her expanding chest promptly brushing along the heel of Josh's hand. Her skin tightened, her breasts puckered in immediate response. Thankfully, her sequins and her starchy strapless bra kept her reactions well hidden.

"I think you'd better explain yourself so we don't misunderstand each other," she managed to say.

He leaned so close that his rough cheek grazed her smooth skin; his lips hovered beside her ear. Other than that, his body didn't touch hers, merely stood at the ready if she wanted to reach out and test those hard masculine planes.

"I'm suggesting we ditch this shindig and explore the possibilities of being chained together in a more private setting."

Her knees liquefied. Her blood simmered at his

words. She had thought if a man paid attention to her tonight it would soothe the wound to her spirit.

She'd been wrong.

Nothing about Josh's provocative proposal soothed her. She'd never been more on edge, more restless, in her life.

He backed up an inch as if to gauge her reaction. His gray eyes locked on her, his face lit by a blue strobe light from the dance floor.

"I can't leave now." Oh, how she wanted to. She'd never been propositioned with anything remotely close to this. If she didn't have any personal magnetism, this man was doing a damn good job of making her feel like she did. An electric charge zinged between them—major sexual attraction.

"Why not?"

She struggled to remember why not. "I have a commitment to the Shelter the Homeless organization." If she didn't do her job to raise money for them, who would? The rest of the partygoers seemed too busy gossiping about her to be of any help.

He peered back at her, silently informing her that her answer hadn't told him what he wanted to know.

Nervousness seized her. She rocked back and forth on her heels to burn off the excess energy pinging through her body. "In fact, I've left the jail cell empty for far too long. If I don't start filling it with prisoners, we'll never raise enough money for the homeless."

When he didn't move, she tugged lightly on his handcuffs. "So, would you mind?"

His jaw flexed and tightened.

Lexi suspected major teeth clenching took place to

warrant such intricate muscle play. Even the diamond stud in his ear shifted in response.

She wondered what it would be like to smooth her fingers over the jaw, trail her tongue over the fiery white diamond.

"No." His terse answer called her from her fantasies.

Irritation replaced a small fraction of the lust frazzling her nerves. "What do you mean, no? You bought a ticket to this event, mister, you can damn well participate in the charitable aspect of the party."

Was Detective Winger one of those guys who never opened his wallet for anything but his own entertainment?

"That's not it. I—"

Before he had a chance to finish his thought, a clipboard nudged between them, followed by a polo shirt decorated with a charity name tag. Event organizer Wendy Garret grinned up at Josh, eyes filled with feminine admiration, and inserted herself in their conversation. A thirty-something political activist with long ties to tonight's charity, Wendy had begged Lexi to champion the event in her column.

"I see you've found your next jailbird, Lex. Good work." The event coordinator's eyes never left Josh.

Lexi managed a smile, struggling to shake off the peculiar feelings Josh had inspired. "Yes, I was just going to lock him up."

Wendy handed Lexi an extra set of cuffs. "Give him to me, and you go find our next victim. We need to turn things over a little faster tonight if we want to meet our goals."

Josh glared at them both. "Look, I'm no celebrity. No one is going to pay ransom for a guy like me."

Lexi clicked off her end of Josh's cuffs and handed them to Wendy. She had a feeling it wouldn't be that simple to oust Josh from her thoughts, however. She'd be thinking about his offer for a long time to come.

"You sorely underestimate yourself," Lexi muttered under her breath. Already, she was debating springing him from that cell herself so they could go back to the fascinating conversation they'd been having about the merits of being locked together.

In those moments with Josh, it hadn't mattered what the rest of the world thought about her. She'd only been able to think about him.

Wendy was already steering Josh toward the stage, a pink blush on her scrubbed cheeks. "Celebrity status doesn't matter. The women bid like crazy on the men. They're much more competitive about this. It's great for us."

Lexi watched them go, telling herself she would not sympathize with a man who wouldn't play his role to help charity. Still, she lingered there, staring at Josh's squared shoulders as he stalked toward the jail cell.

Who was she kidding? She'd gladly chain herself to Josh Winger, Scrooge or not.

He'd made it clear he wanted her, something no other man had ever managed to articulate. Sure, she could tick off a couple of one-night stands she'd indulged in, just to experience sex for herself. But she'd been the aggressor then, and she'd run like an Olympic sprinter the morning after, to be sure those men never saw her again.

This man wanted *her*.

Too bad she'd only had to handcuff him to secure the admission.

Ignoring the ego-deflating realization, Lexi now found it easy to shut out the gossip-filled club.

She knew her sexy quarry would be long gone by the time she finished her stint as jailer tonight, and oddly, that knowledge stung more than the shredding of her reputation.

IMPRISONED by a five-foot dominatrix—a hell of a way to start undercover police work.

Of course, this job was no longer undercover. All of New York's fashion bigwigs would know him on sight after tonight.

Josh gnashed his teeth a few more times for good measure, knowing he'd blow a gasket if he didn't get out of the jail cell soon. Who would have thought he'd be staring out from the wrong side of prison bars tonight?

No doubt it would probably help his chances of escape if he smiled at some of the coiffed and manicured socialites who peered into his cage, but he was too angry with himself to work up the energy.

He should have just told Lexi Mansfield he wished to remain anonymous, instead of whispering seductive suggestions in her ear to distract her from her purpose. He'd been the one who ended up preoccupied, while she had remained committed to her charitable cause. What had he been thinking of, to proposition her when he had work to do?

Josh wasn't the type of guy who allowed himself to get distracted. The one time he'd lost focus on a job had resulted in a death he'd regret the rest of his days and a scandal that rocked the city. Josh knew better now.

He ran his life with rigid control. He made choices with careful deliberation. And he sure as hell didn't spend his Saturday nights behind bars.

Damn.

Glaring out into the crowd, he searched for Lexi. She'd already brought four other "prisoners" to jail, all of whom had been released. Josh had inadvertently scared off all the women who'd been interested in ransoming him, probably because he'd been snarling in his frustration at blowing his objectives tonight.

The only person who didn't seem intimidated by his scowl was Lexi. The feisty jail keeper made sure to send him a wink every time she delivered a new hostage to captivity, unruffled by Josh's surly mien.

He caught sight of her sashaying his way again, this time with a guy big enough to be a linebacker in tow. The strobe lights flashed over the silver handcuffs between them, a winking reminder that Lexi had probably flirted her way into bondage with half the men in the bar tonight.

The thought made him gnash his teeth all over again. Why should he give a rip that Lexi liked playing love-slave games?

She reached the cell door and inserted an oversize key into the padlock. "Still here, Detective?" she called, quirking a brow in his direction. "You could have raised a small fortune for us with that sexy bod of yours if you hadn't glowered at every woman who dared to look at you," she chided. "Want me to send you over another whiskey to help loosen you up?"

She waved her new prisoner into the cell and removed the guy's cuffs.

Josh fought the urge to throttle the big lug. Why did he have to stand half an inch from Lexi? "The whiskey isn't what I need."

The linebacker folded his arms over his chest and frowned down at their jailer. "I thought you told me you didn't talk to the captives, Lex. How come you talk to this guy?"

That caught Josh's attention. Did Lexi treat the other male captives differently than she'd treated him? Maybe he didn't feel so throttle-happy, after all.

Lexi looked sheepish for all of an instant, casting a wary glance at Josh before she answered. "Your wife would call me out if I so much as breathed the same air as you, Alec, and you know it. New brides can be very protective."

The linebacker grinned the goofy guy-in-love grin Josh had seen on his partner's face too many times the past month. "Shoot, Lexi, Nina likes you just fine."

Lexi twirled the handcuffs around her finger, watching the silver rings spin under the flashes of colored light. Did the woman ever sit still? She was a riot of nervous energy even when her feet stopped moving. Maybe that's why Josh couldn't seem to take his eyes off her and her sequins tonight.

Yeah, right.

On instinct, Josh reached out and snatched the handcuffs off her finger, halting her motion for a moment. Lexi's startled gaze moved over him, her mouth forming a surprised ''O'' with her lips.

Josh had an image of her in his bed, her body still beneath him in the moment before a climax hit her. She would look just like this.

Too soon, she resumed her flurry of movement, yanking her handcuffs back and spinning on one high heel.

''I'll thank you not to steal those, Mr. High-and-Mighty Detective.'' She stuck her tongue out at him as she secured the lock on the cell door. ''You'll have to find your own handcuffs to play with.''

The sight of that small, pink tongue would torment him the rest of the night. ''But where will I find my own captive?'' Josh could hear Alec the linebacker chuckling in the background.

Lexi flipped her hands out, palms up, in an exaggerated shrug. ''Since you blew your chances with all the ladies here tonight, it looks like you're stuck being my prisoner.''

He crooked his finger at her, beckoning her closer.

She hesitated for a moment, then boldly stepped forward. Josh had the feeling this woman wouldn't back down easily.

She waited just outside the cell bars, her black sequins close enough to touch. She tapped her foot on the dark commercial carpet, unable to stand still for a minute.

Josh reached one finger through the bars to trail

down her bare arm. He watched, fascinated, as a path of chill bumps appeared in his wake.

"I don't mind being your prisoner, honey, but couldn't we play this out somewhere else? Like your place, maybe?" He kept his voice low enough that only she could hear. What did it matter if he let himself get a little distracted by Lexi now? He sure as hell wasn't going to gain anything for his investigation from inside this cell.

Maybe she thought about it. She stilled for a moment and watched him with a predatory interest that made him want to rattle the damn cage.

Then she folded her arms over her chest and stepped back. "Sorry, I don't fraternize with the inmates. Especially not the ones who refuse to play the game."

"Lex, I'm ready to play whatever games you have in mind."

He couldn't be sure in the dim light, but he thought he actually made her blush.

"I don't need you to play *those* kinds of games, wise guy. I needed you to turn that sexy charm on any one of the umpteen hot and bothered ladies who filed past your cell tonight. You couldn't have done your part to help the homeless?"

Words escaped him. She looked seriously offended.

"Sorry, Lexi." He couldn't exactly explain to her his reasons. At least, not now. How had the dominatrix gone from turning him on, to making him feel like the world's biggest heel in ten seconds flat? "Let me ransom myself to make up for it, and I'll buy you a drink."

She frowned. "Too many drinks made me cuff you in the first place. Why don't you just cool your heels for a little longer and maybe I'll ransom you, if you can remember not to snarl at anyone else."

He smoothed his tie and straightened his lapels. "I'm working for time off with good behavior, honey, and I'll pay you back for your trouble."

A ghost of a smile played around her lips. Josh found himself eager to see that saucy grin again.

"I'll be sure to collect, Winger."

She sauntered off with a definite swing to her sequined hips.

Apparently he wasn't the only one who noticed, because his cell mate emitted a long, low whistle.

Josh bristled. "The wiggle was meant for my eyes, Jack."

The linebacker shook his head, grinning. "It's Alec. And sorry, man, but I'm not blind."

"Don't you have a wife around here somewhere?" Josh wondered if he could keep his word about not snarling.

"Yep. She's probably too busy dishing about Lexi to come bust me out of here, though."

Josh frowned. "What do you mean?" Lexi might be a little flirtatious, but she didn't exactly seem like the home-wrecking type.

"You know, all that garbage they said about Lex in her magazine today. The women can't get enough of it." Alec shrugged his big shoulders and pulled a face.

Protective instincts roared to life. "A magazine article about Lexi?" Josh knew how it felt to have his personal life splashed all over the headlines—most of it untrue. Had Lexi been subjected to that?

"She's not your girl?"

"Not yet." The words sprang forth before Josh had the chance to consciously form them. He definitely wasn't in the market for a relationship. Then again, he couldn't picture not seeing Lexi again. "But we seem to have…hit it off."

"You know that fashion magazine she reviews for?" Alec slumped against the cell bars.

Josh didn't, but he nodded. He didn't want to seem like some joker hitting on Lexi without knowing a damn thing about her.

"Well, the magazine ran a letter to the editor today that trashed Lexi's column and suggested she's out of date, out of style, whatever." Alec shook his head. "A bunch of catfight-type stuff. The women are gossiping about it a mile a minute, all gunning for Lexi. It's all I've heard all damn night."

"Catfight stuff—but not anything serious, right?" The cop in him snapped to alert as Josh realized he might be in over his head in the fashion world. The waters were murky for him, and now that his partner and his socialite fiancée were taking off for a motorcycle trip this weekend, Josh would be losing his only insider information for a few days.

"Nah. The woman who wrote the letter isn't even here tonight. Besides, this isn't exactly the sort of crowd to take potshots in a dark alley. They do their mud-slinging right in the public eye."

Before Josh could thank the man, Alec sprang to

his feet and smoothed his hair back, his gaze focused outside the cage.

Josh turned to see a scowling blonde barreling toward them, her snappy walk at odds with her elegant white gown. No doubt, Nina had arrived.

Josh mulled over Alec's words as the man's wife ransomed him and the couple left together. As the crowd in the bar thinned out and the dance floor began to clear, Josh wondered if Lexi had attended the fund-raiser with anyone or was here by herself.

Like it or not, he wouldn't allow her to leave the bar by herself. No matter what Alec said about the fashion world slinging their mud in public, Josh didn't like the idea of Lexi being the target of mean-spirited comments. No telling when professional jealousy could get out of hand.

An image of Tonya Harding flashed through his mind, along with the Texas cheerleader's mom. Lexi could be at risk, for all he knew.

He'd just make sure she got home okay, then he would leave.

Unless, of course, he could lure out the *other* side of Lexi—the sequined spitfire who had handcuffed him earlier.

Josh had the feeling that if he tangled with her again, he wouldn't leave until they'd uncovered every erotic possibility of handcuffs.

3

SHE COULDN'T put it off any longer.

Last call had come and gone. Wendy sat at the bar, reviewing the final bill with the property manager. The house lights would probably switch on at any moment.

Lexi had to free her last captive.

Her gaze skittered over to the jail cell where Detective Winger sat on the cage's lone bench. His jacket was draped over the seat beside him, his white shirt stretching over shoulders that delineated mouthwatering muscles. His elbows were propped on his knees, and his silver-gray tie fell forward, the knot loosened long ago.

Lexi didn't need to see his eyes to know the tie matched their color. She'd caught his hungry stare enough times tonight to remember the precise shade.

Squeezing the key to the cell padlock in her fist, she debated her approach. She'd flirted outrageously with Josh all night. Did he expect to cash in on that flirtation? Or would he flag a cab and disappear?

Lexi wasn't sure which idea bothered her more.

She desperately wanted to test her feminine wiles on this man—to assuage the fear that she was as outdated and boring as the scathing letter to her editor had claimed.

But if she went home with him, she needed to make it clear *she* was in charge. She didn't need a man in her life to mess up the comfortable niche she had finally managed to carve for herself. Lexi had struggled for her independence, her self-reliance. As long as Josh understood that, as long as he let her take the lead, everything would be fine.

Lexi hitched up her sequined bodice, fluffed the few tendrils of hair around her face, and approached the jail cell.

Her steps faltered when Josh stood. He topped her by nearly a foot. The reminder of that height, those big shoulders, did funny things to her insides.

He scooped up his jacket and slid it on again. "Am I free to go?"

Lexi swallowed in a fruitless attempt to cure her suddenly dry mouth. "You're getting your time off for good behavior." She unlocked the cell door and stood back to allow him out. "I haven't seen you snarl in at least an hour."

He didn't step past her, however. He stopped right in front of her and startled her with his direct gaze. "I can be well behaved if the situation calls for it."

She felt the blush starting, and resisted the urge to fan herself. The man wreaked havoc on her internal cooling system.

And amazingly, rendered her speechless.

She wasn't sure if she wanted Josh to be well behaved or not, but the idea that he would be "good" if she wanted him to, left her mute for an agonizing moment.

He reached for her. But instead of pulling him toward her for the kiss she sorely wanted, he gently tugged one of the fallen tendrils from her upswept hair. Slowly, he wound the long strand around his finger.

He studied her with restless gray eyes. "How are you getting home?"

The question jarred her out of her reverie. She didn't know how to respond to his blunt question, especially since she'd rather hoped to go home with him. Still, she didn't want to look too eager.

"I can walk from here."

She lived just around the corner, but her place was off-limits. The two times she had worked up the courage to proposition a man—the only one-nighters she'd ever had—she'd made sure they went to his place.

Josh frowned. "You can't walk."

Lexi bristled. Josh might be gorgeous, but he was not in charge here. "Of course I can walk. I live nearby."

He steered her forward with a gentle hand at her waist and looked as if he hadn't heard her. "Where's your coat? I'll take you home."

She stopped in her tracks. "I don't think so."

"I'd try to talk you into coming home with me, but my apartment is in the middle of being repainted. We can't go there."

Heat bothered her cheeks. "Of course not. I didn't

mean to suggest we would. I'll be fine heading home on my own."

His mouth set in a straight, hard line. For the first time, Lexi noticed a scar on his cheekbone, a thin white line that seemed more prominent when he scowled.

"Lexi, I'm a cop. You're a half-dressed woman ready to roam the streets of New York at two in the morning. Sorry, but I'm pulling rank here."

She felt her jaw slacken and promptly snapped it shut. "You, sir, are obviously blind. Don't you dare suggest that wearing a Bill Blass original is anything less than being completely and flawlessly dressed." She'd sooner crawl home than allow anyone to cast one more aspersion on her character today. She'd deflected jibes and gossip this evening like a damn mud flap.

Josh scrubbed a hand over his chest before sliding his palm down the length of his silk tie. "You took a lot of crap here tonight?"

She stilled. "What would you know about that?"

"Alec told me about the magazine piece."

Great. Now the stud of her dreams felt sorry for her. "A letter to the editor by some disgruntled designer is not the end of the world." Or so she told herself. Repeatedly.

He shrugged. "I don't keep up with the fashion magazines, I guess. But I don't like the idea of you taking off by yourself after being the target of so much slander here tonight."

Slander. Yes, she rather liked the ring of that. She

sniffed. "I guess it wouldn't hurt if you walked me home."

"Great." He headed toward the cloakroom. "What does your coat look like?"

"Black pashmina."

His brow furrowed, but he ducked into the room and out of sight.

Damn. Now she wouldn't be able to seduce him. There would be no night in Josh's arms to chase away the cold loneliness she'd felt all day because she would *not* let him in her apartment...would she?

Of course not. What would all her pets think? They wouldn't want to share their mama with some strange man. And she'd always promised herself not to spoil the sanctuary of her home by allowing a man inside. It had been different to sleep in someone else's bed. Impersonal. Easy to distance herself the next day.

But Josh would be a difficult man to walk away from, in the first place. She sure as heck couldn't let him into the private world where the *real* Lexi lived.

"Is it a black blanket?" he called from the cloakroom. He stepped out with her pashmina in hand, a frustrated glower on his face.

"That's me." Laughing, she walked to the bar and tugged her purse from a shelf the bartender had allowed her to use.

Josh closed the distance between them in a flash. "Why didn't you say so?"

His gruff manners soothed her as he wrapped the cashmere shawl around her and tugged the ends tightly shut.

"How the hell do you wear this thing?"

Smothering a giggle, she flung one end over her shoulder in demonstration.

Josh muttered an oath under his breath and tried to tuck the other end under her arm. Having secured every loose corner of the shawl, he nodded. "There. Don't move."

"How am I going to walk home?"

He grinned. "Guess I'll have to carry you."

Warmth pooled low in her belly at the thought of her body tucked up against his. Part of her longed to assume her flirtatious guise and maneuver more sexy talk with him. But some of her daring had faded along with the buzz from that last cosmopolitan. Even worse, she liked Josh more by the minute—a fact that rendered a one-night stand less appealing. A torrid night with Josh practically guaranteed she'd never see him again.

She shook loose his handiwork and rewrapped the shawl. "I don't think that's the best idea."

He snorted. "Let's look at who's coming up with the good ideas here tonight. You think it's a good idea to traipse around New York alone at 2:00 a.m. I think it's a good idea for us to leave together. You think it's a good idea to put me in jail. I think it's a good idea for us to explore the possibilities of being—"

She hurried to cut him off. "I get the picture." She definitely didn't need reminders of his earlier provocative suggestion. Handcuffs had never seemed so appealing. But she needed to put some distance between her and Josh before he got the wrong idea. No matter how much her hormones argued the fact, she could not sleep with Josh in her apartment. "But I'm not conceding the point. I still think my ideas have been very sensible."

Sensible. The word resounded in Josh's mind, at odds with everything he thought about Lexi Mansfield. "Is that what you want, Lexi? Sensible?"

She deftly unfastened the diamond collar around her throat and slid it into a tiny purse she carried. "See that? Sensible. I may occasionally carry handcuffs and go manhunting on the posh New York club scene, Josh, but I'm not crazy enough to wear Harry Winston out in public."

Josh stared at the long, smooth column of bare neck the diamonds had just vacated. She suddenly looked less like his five-foot dominatrix and more like a vulnerable woman.

"I never suggested you were crazy." Josh curled his arm around her back and ushered her toward the door. Lexi flung good-nights and smiles at the few remaining people they passed on their way out. He hoped the high color in her cheeks had something to do with his touch.

As he held the door for her, she looked up at him and paused. "Are you sure?"

"A little wild maybe, but definitely not crazy."

She nodded as if satisfied and walked out onto Columbus Circle, the black blanket fluttering in her wake.

Josh followed close behind, surveying the activity on the street. They were near Lincoln Center in a great neighborhood, but Central Park loomed to one side—and who knew what might leap out of the bushes at this time of night.

"Do you really live right around the corner, or were you just hoping I'd let you go home alone?"

She fidgeted on her high heels and pointed. "West Sixty-second Street. You can almost see the blue awning from here."

He squinted. The buildings in this neighborhood all had doormen and good security, but that didn't mean she couldn't get jumped from an alleyway. "I guess we can walk. But you really should take cabs at night if you're by yourself."

"And pay five bucks to go two blocks? No, thank you." She set the pace as her high heels clicked down the pavement.

Josh smiled to himself as he noticed she took two steps to his one, her slim dress limiting her stride to a sexy little walk.

He fell into step beside her, fighting the urge to sling a protective arm around her.

Would she mind? She'd definitely backed off the flirting ever since he'd insisted he would walk her home. Had he misread her signals? After Lexi's prolonged pursuit at the club and her teasing overtures with the handcuffs, Josh had been pretty certain she would be amenable to spending the night with him. Now he wasn't so sure.

He would walk away if she wanted him to, of course. But he didn't relish the idea. He'd had hours in the jail cell to resign himself to the fact that he wouldn't be getting any work done on his investigation tonight. His work for the night had been compromised, but not his overall case. Once he'd come to terms with a night off, he'd gladly spent the rest of the time indulging in erotic fantasies about Lexi.

He had another block and a half to sway the odds in his favor, and he didn't plan to waste them lecturing her about street safety.

The night air was crisp and clear. A few fall leaves barely clung to the trees planted at precise intervals along the street. A light breeze caught stray strands of Lexi's hair.

Josh racked his brain for the right approach. He didn't usually have to work at this—the women in his past had made it known they were available. He'd thought Lexi was like that, too, but she was turning out to be more complicated than he'd expected.

Didn't matter.

He wanted her more than he could remember wanting any other woman.

He brushed his hand over her shoulder. "You warm enough in that thing?"

She slanted him a sideways glance. "Plenty warm."

"You ever share your blankets?" He tugged one corner of her shawl and crossed his fingers.

She stared straight ahead. "No."

Her heels clicked down the street, ticking off his remaining time to seduce her. The odds seemed to be going up in her favor with every step she took.

Click.

Click.

Click.

"So Alec told me you write reviews for a magazine." He might as well find out a little about her. He didn't see how any great Casanova move would salvage his night with the dominatrix, anyway.

Oddly enough, he wanted to learn more about her even though he knew she'd be sending him home soon.

"It's *New York Fashion* magazine. I've been writing the style column for five years, now." She unearthed her hands from the mass of black cashmere and huffed warm breath on them.

Josh watched the steam rise from her folded palms, plagued by a vague sense that he'd seen her somewhere before tonight. She had a familiar smile....

She peered over at him, pausing just before they reached her awning. "Just how much did Alec tell you about me?"

Josh took her hands in his and tugged her to the side of the street. He must be wrong thinking she looked like someone he'd met before. "He told me the women were giving you a hard time tonight."

He wrapped his hands around hers, then pulled their knot of fingers toward his lips. Mirroring her actions of a moment before, he huffed a slow, heated breath over her cool skin.

"I can manage myself," Lexi said, her voice halting just a little. She didn't pull away. "I mean, a lot of those people at the party were designers or else they work with a design house. Because I critique their work, I'm sure at one point or another over the past few years I've offended almost everyone."

Her eyes were huge in the dim light from a street lamp. Josh wanted nothing so much as to wrap her cashmere blanket around both of them and pull her to him. He could envision every nuance of her sequined curves and he longed to test the knowledge of his eyes with his hands. Would she feel as good as she looked?

"That doesn't make it okay for them to gang up on you tonight. It had to be awkward for you." He settled for curving one hand along her jaw and brushing the soft silk of her cheek with his thumb.

"A little." She half sighed the words, giving Josh the impression her thoughts lay elsewhere. Lexi's eyes closed for a moment, then flew open again.

Josh wanted to shout over that small victory.

She took a small step away, her hands still tangled with one of his. "I'd better get going."

"Let me just walk you to your door." He kept one of her hands in his and wrapped his other arm lightly around her waist.

"I don't think you need to—"

Josh nodded at the doorman and hustled her inside her building. "I'll feel better knowing you're safe."

She pushed the elevator button and turned to stare up at him. "Who's going to keep me safe from you?"

"You want me to put the cuffs back on?"

A blush stained her cheeks. She twisted one of her rings in a relentless circle around her finger. "Um. No. That's okay."

The elevator slid open and Lexi stepped inside.

Josh waited at the doors. "I mean it, Lex. You shouldn't get into an elevator with a guy you don't trust." He pulled out his badge and flashed it at her.

"You know, you never verified that I really am a cop."

With a nervous glance toward the doorman, Lexi reached out and pulled Josh forward by his tie. "I trust you," she hissed.

The door swished shut behind them.

"I wouldn't have let you walk me home if I thought you were the kind of guy to leave me for dead," she assured him.

"Well, that's a hell of an endorsement." It's not like he was going to try to talk her into anything.

But he sensed a kiss in their future, damn it, and he hadn't wanted to indulge in that particular experience in full view of Sixty-second Street.

Lexi heard the grumbling note in his voice and wondered if she'd offended him. She hadn't meant to.

Strangely, she did trust him. If he had meant to hurt her, he wouldn't have knuckled under to her flirtatious handcuff job at the bar. He'd cooled his heels in her jail cell for hours, and still wanted to walk her home.

It was herself she didn't trust.

Josh's big, solid presence had her pulse racing and her fingers itching to touch him. When he'd taken her hands in his and breathed over her skin, she'd nearly shot right out of her shoes.

Her mind had fast-forwarded to all sorts of scenarios that involved Josh's breath on her flesh. She wanted to taste him, breathe him, explore every inch of that muscular body...but she wouldn't.

Not here. Not on her home turf.

It would give the whole encounter way too much

significance. She'd never be able to sleep in her bed again with the same sense of peace. She'd never be able to feel like the queen of her own palace again. There would be a man's shadow cast over her kingdom, a fear that maybe the world she'd built for herself wasn't enough.

And she would not allow that to happen.

When the elevator doors opened on the twelfth floor, Lexi stepped out, willing her heart to slow down a few notches.

"I'm this way," she said, digging her keys out of her purse. She wondered if her four-legged babies would hear her coming down the hall or if they were all fast asleep.

She stopped at the door of her apartment, not hearing any telltale barks. Maybe she'd be able to visit with Josh for a minute, to at least smooth things over with him, as long as her pets seemed settled.

"Thanks for the escort," she said, her gaze bouncing all over the deserted hallway, lighting anywhere but on him.

"My pleasure."

He stood close enough to remind her of his potent effect, but not so close that she felt crowded.

She twirled one fringed end of her shawl and searched for a way to end things on a light note. "I mean, I'm not afraid to make the walk by myself, but I'll admit it's sort of cool to trek around the city with my own bodyguard."

His gray eyes narrowed. A silver light glittered in their depths. "Maybe you ought to put your body in my hands a little more often."

Lexi backed up a step, his soft words a deft blow to her defenses. She felt an answering simmer in her veins, a heat that bubbled just below the surface. "That might be a bit of a risk."

He edged closer, stealing her breath along with her thoughts. He placed one hand on either side of her, bracketing her against her apartment door. The dominant position made Lexi think about lying beneath him in her bed, his arms levering him above her body as he made love to her.

"Honey, you just let me take all the risks. I'm here to take care of your body, remember?"

She breathed his scent—smoke and scotch from the bar, but some sort of soapy scent, too—and fought for her balance. She hadn't been this close to a man for nearly two years.

And being close to this particular man was a test of self-discipline Lexi wasn't sure she could pass.

She'd picked him out at the bar because he had a reckless sort of look, a hint of danger that had appealed to her daring mood.

Only she wasn't feeling so daring now. And in spite of that badge, Josh Winger was proving every bit as dangerous as she'd imagined.

"Josh?" All she had to do was tell him good-night. She steeled herself to send him away, to end the heat wave on the twelfth floor.

Too bad she looked up to find his gaze focused on her mouth.

"Hmm?" His answer sounded as distracted as she felt.

She swallowed, battling the urge to just close her eyes. No words came.

She licked her lips in a renewed effort to speak. Too late, she realized her mistake.

The strangled noise he made in his throat wavered between a growl and a groan, a hungry sound that rumbled right through her in the moment before his mouth met hers.

Her lips parted on a welcoming sigh, her little moan of delight sounding foreign to her ears.

Hints of a five-o'clock shadow gone rogue scraped her chin and cheeks. His tongue teased over hers in a stroke of warm velvet. The fire she'd been playing with ever since she'd spotted him leapt out of control—inside her body and out.

The whiskey taste of him drugged her until his hungry mouth went questing down her throat. She shivered at the wet heat of the kiss, and wriggled her way closer to the hard wall of his chest.

Josh's hands fell away from the door to hold her against him. He stroked his way down her spine, sealing her body to his with each new inch of sequined territory. His arousal nudged her belly and fed her imagination, making her want to drag him inside and indulge herself in him.

She thought about dropping her purse and her keys so she could run her hands all over him, soak in the feel of him through her fingertips.

Before she had a chance, he pried himself away.

Lexi blinked, confused.

"Honey, I need to know if this is what you want."

She didn't have to ask what "this" was. "This"

currently strained against her, sizzling her from the outside in.

Somewhere in the passion fog of her brain, she heard a dog bark. For the first time in her life, she didn't want to run inside to greet her pets.

She wanted this man, this feeling, this renewed sense of daring to last all night long. She'd figure out how to handle the backlash tomorrow, when her hormones weren't conspiring against her.

Right now, all she could think of was finishing the game she'd started in the bar.

Lexi wriggled against him shamelessly. "Don't make me break out the handcuffs again, Detective. You're not going anywhere tonight."

4

HANDCUFFS *and* a sex goddess. The fates had granted Josh all his best fantasies in one feisty package called Lexi Mansfield.

Lust surged through him with renewed force. Lexi had just given him the green light.

He withdrew her apartment keys from her fingers, eager to proceed inside before she changed her mind. Women like Lexi didn't come along every day, at least not in the world Josh lived in. His usual dates were women he'd met at the gym, women who wanted the same things from a relationship he did— physical release and a simple good time. Josh had no complaints about those relationships, but he wasn't about to let anything mess up his chance to play bondage games with a spitfire dominatrix.

He'd barely pushed his way inside Lexi's apartment when a pack of wild dogs rushed him. The restrained barks he'd heard a few moments ago turned into a chorus of raucous canine yipping and howling. Josh couldn't see the animals in Lexi's darkened foyer, but he could hear the snapping jaws, glimpse the flashes of white teeth around his knees.

"That's enough, guys," Lexi admonished, somehow managing to shoo the brood down a short hallway. "You can play in the guest room while Mama has company."

As the barking died down, Josh became aware of a bird chirping in the background. The hum of a fish tank circulator provided a soft white noise, drawing his eye toward a small aquarium and the lone source of light in the room. One pink fish swam around bright cliffs of coral in its home on the kitchen counter.

Distracted by the menagerie, Josh failed to notice Lexi's return until she was a few feet in front of him. He couldn't distinguish all the particulars, but he could tell she'd ditched her high heels somewhere along the way. Not only had she grown quieter, but also she'd lost a few inches. Josh guessed if he pulled her close her head would just reach his shoulder.

"Sorry about that."

Wariness threaded through her words. Hesitation. Second thoughts.

"Not a problem." He stepped closer, looking for ways to gain lost ground. He had a hunch that if he struck out with Lexi tonight, there wouldn't be any second chance. Her house full of pets had him thinking she wasn't the sort of woman who lived on the edge very often.

Normally when he brought a woman home from the gym or the boxing club, he would simply initiate a carnal wrestling match that would leave them both breathless and more than satisfied. But he got the impression Lexi was the kind of woman who wouldn't appreciate the erotic possibilities of a half nelson.

"The animals miss me when I go out." She traced

her toe along one of the floorboards in the foyer, her body backlit by the blue glow of the fish tank. "They're excited to see me."

"I can hardly blame them." Josh nudged aside the folds of her black shawl to trace one finger along the delicate ridge of her collarbone. "Just standing next to you makes me feel like howling."

Her heartbeat pounded just below the heel of his hand.

"Don't tell me I'm going to have to lock you up in the guest bedroom, too."

He smoothed his hand over her shoulder and allowed his fingers to skim along her back. "I think I could better serve you if you'd lock me up in *your* bedroom."

She couldn't hide her answering shiver. Josh felt it right through his fingertips. Nevertheless, she shook her head resolutely.

"Sorry. I've seen how much you resent captivity. I'm not going to make that mistake again."

Josh heard the underlying message, despite the haze of lust that had him in a chokehold. He paused his fingertip exploration of her back, unwilling to use sensual means to get his own way tonight.

"Lexi, are you uncomfortable with me being here?" He wanted this woman more than he'd wanted anything in recent memory. Make that long-term memory. But he wanted her at full speed, all or nothing, as hungry for him as he was for her. He searched her face for some clue to her real feelings.

Damn it, but she looked familiar to him. Still, he

would remember having met a woman like Lexi. He had to be mistaken.

The fish tank burbled softly, while he waited. The chirping bird in the background provided an obnoxiously happy accompaniment.

"You want to know the truth?" Finally, she tossed her shawl aside and planted jeweled fists on her hips.

In his mind's eye he saw her donning boxing gloves, preparing for the round in which she would deliver the knockout blow—the "go home" speech.

"Nothing but the truth," he returned, realizing he meant it. He didn't want a sugarcoated speech from this woman. "Why don't you tell me exactly what you want."

Her eyebrows lifted in surprise, then slowly settled back into place as her gaze narrowed.

"Then, I'll tell you exactly what I want, Josh Winger." She spun on her bare heel and stalked into the living room. Now that his eyes had adjusted to the subdued light of the fish tank he could see her toenails were painted bright blue.

"I want a man to take me seriously for once." She folded her arms over her compact body, a body visibly thrumming with an emotion he couldn't fully identify. "For that matter, I would settle for *anyone* taking me seriously for once."

"Well—"

Before he could respond, she burst into motion again, stomping around her living room sofa to pose by her coffee table. "I mean, look at me. Why can't anyone appreciate the fashion sense I impart to all of New York? I know how to be tasteful and refined."

She pointed a finger in his direction and then started a slow trek back to him. "The point is, I don't allow myself to fall into a rut of the refined but boring clothes that we've seen done to death for the past decade."

He was so far out of his element he might as well have been swimming in the tank with the damn fish.

"I think you really look great—"

"I am willing to take risks, and that's what no one seems to understand." In the course of her emphatic speech, a few more locks of hair slipped free of the knot on top of her head. He was trying to follow what she was saying, damn it, but thoughts of unpinning that hair and seeing how much of her body it would cover was more than a little distracting.

"I might mix a few over-the-top colors, and I admit that my go-go boots with the Gucci cocktail dress was a definite mistake, but the point is, I push the boundaries." By now, she stood toe to toe with him. "I am willing to try something different in order to create something unique and beautiful."

She gazed up at him, eyes so dark they looked like a doll's—all one color, with no hint of where the pupil ended and the iris began.

Clearly, the time had arrived for him to speak.

"I am definitely willing to try something different," he said, trying to steer the conversation back toward bedrooms and handcuffs.

By the defeated slope of her shoulders he sensed that wasn't the right thing to do.

Damn.

He scratched his head in the vain hope of stimulating a few coherent thoughts, and took a final stab at it. "But I understand what you're saying. About taking risks, I mean."

Her hip cocked to one side as she shifted her weight. The stance broadcast her skepticism more loudly than if she'd rolled her eyes, but at least she was listening.

"Like tonight, for example. I took a risk by not running to the tuxedo shop for the monkey suit I was supposed to have worn. The dinner jacket was a risk, as was the earring. But I'm not the kind of guy who makes concessions easily."

He hoped that was a smile playing along the line of her mouth.

"But, like you, I know when to play it safe, too. I knew enough to grab the shiny silver tie out of my closet instead of the red-striped one. Shiny silver says I can bow to convention when I need to, right?"

Lexi laughed. Was this guy for real? Any other man would have run screaming for her door at the first mention of fashion. Then again, there was nothing ordinary about Josh Winger. She stepped closer to trail her fingers down the tie in question.

"Maybe we do have a few things in common," she admitted, enjoying the way her fingernails rasped against the crisp cotton of his shirt. "But as much as I would like for something to happen between us tonight, I'm still not sure."

She'd broken every rule of smart dating by letting a guy she barely knew inside her apartment and then telling him no. But she trusted Josh on a gut level, and she had always been the kind of woman to let her instincts guide her.

"What do you need to make you feel sure?"

His words were surprisingly gentle, coming from a man who looked like he could have been cast as a mobster in a shoot-'em-up flick.

"I felt more ready to be with you when I thought things could remain sort of impersonal." She knew she had to stop touching him, had to take a step back from his big, sexy body. But the planes of his chest fascinated her, called to her, wouldn't let her stop the fingertip massage of all those male muscles.

"You're afraid of getting too personal?"

There was a hoarse edge to his voice that made her wonder if her touch affected him as much as it did her.

She nodded, not trusting her own voice.

He gripped her wrists in his palms, lightly restraining her. "That feels phenomenal, but I can't think straight when you touch me like that."

Feminine pride curled through her, even though he seemed to have no idea he'd just paid her a compliment. She whispered a mental "in your face" to all her detractors tonight.

Houseplant be damned. She must have some magnetism left somewhere, to be able to distract this man.

Josh closed his eyes while keeping her wrists imprisoned. He tilted his head back, just a little, exposing to her view the thick cords of muscle in his neck.

Then he looked down, his eyelids snapping open. "I've got it."

Gray eyes locked on to hers, startling her out of

her contemplation. "You do?" She wondered if he was going to let go of her wrists. Part of her didn't want him to.

"Anonymous sex."

Her heart skipped a beat. Maybe several.

When it started again, it pumped erratically, awkwardly.

"Excuse me?"

Josh relinquished his hold on her wrists, allowing her arms to drop to her sides. Nothing resided between them now except a sizzling two inches of air.

"You don't want to make it personal, so we'll make it anonymous." His gray eyes glittered down at her, looming nearer as he closed the distance between them. "No lights." His mouth brushed hers with a featherlight sweep of his lips. "No conversation." He kissed his way across her jaw to whisper in her ear. "Just you and me—" he trailed his finger down her shoulder to her elbow "—tangled in your sheets until dawn."

Lexi didn't know when her eyes had drifted shut, but she found herself fantasizing about that simple touch winding its way down her belly, or maybe her thighs.

The imagined caress turned into a very real one as Josh brought his fingertip to rest in the middle of her cheek. He skimmed it along her jaw and down her neck. Slowly.

"So, what do you say?"

She pried open her eyelids, needing to look at him when she made this decision. If she kept her eyes closed, she would agree to anything. Everything.

"I don't know." Her voice was breathy, hungry. "It seems a little…"

"Risky?"

Yes. But not in the way he thought. Lexi trusted this dangerous-looking police detective to protect her tonight. What she didn't trust was her ability to forget about him in the morning. And becoming attached to this man was a definite risk.

Still, Lexi didn't want to spend another night sleeping with Muffin, as much as she adored her miniature poodle.

She couldn't let this perfect opportunity slip away, not when she wanted it so badly.

"We've already established that I don't have a problem with taking risks."

Josh nodded slowly, thoughtfully. "Yes, but we've also established you can play it safe and conservative when the situation calls for it."

Damn it, how could a night with this guy ever be impersonal? He already knew more about her than a city full of her devoted readers.

She pointed one finger into the muscular wall of his chest, needing to take charge of this situation before it got out of control.

"Well, this is not one of those times, hot stuff."

JOSH COULD TELL by the wicked gleam in Lexi's eyes that the dynamo he'd met at the bar was back to play.

"You're ready to take a risk, then?" His sense of fairness wanted her to spell it out for him. Despite the dangerous reputation he'd gained in his years on the police force, he wasn't the kind of guy who could burn up the sheets with a stranger without knowing the stranger in question was one hundred percent into the game.

"The bedroom is that way, tiger." She gripped his tie in her fist and backed him up a step.

Green lights flashed in front of his eyes.

"With pleasure." He allowed her to back him right into a closed door.

He reached for the knob to let them in, but Lexi was too close, too hot, too fierce.

"With pleasure…is that a promise?" She plastered herself against him—thighs, hips, breasts—and snaked her arms around his shoulders.

She smelled like a hothouse—feminine and exotic, but she was no delicate flower. Despite her petite size, Lexi possessed surprising strength. Her slender muscles were toned and defined, as if she'd logged more than a few hours at the gym. And she held him against the door with the force of a rookie cop with something to prove.

"Lady, I'd make it a blood oath if you want me to." He shifted his weight underneath her, situating one thigh between hers.

Her thighs hugged him, invited him to dare even more.

She shook her head, dislodging a few more long locks of hair. "I believe you."

He lifted his fingers to the mass of black hair and tunneled through the soft strands in a mad search for pins. He found a single smooth stick piercing the center of the knot and pulled it free.

A riot of silky black waves tumbled down to her

shoulders and spilled over her back and breasts, down to her waist. The scent of her shampoo wafted through the air.

"Wow." He wanted to wrap himself in that hair, wrap her in that hair. Run his fingers over every last glossy curl.

She blew a stray strand out of one eye, pursing her lips in a pucker that nearly sent him over the edge.

"It's a little outdated, but I hate getting it cut." She plucked the stick from his hands and tossed it to the floor, heedless of where it landed.

"I like outdated. Outdated is sexy." Josh reached for the doorknob and turned it, backing them into her bedroom. All the while, he kept every inch of her sequined body glued to his.

He paused when the backs of his legs ran into her bed.

"Not here," she whispered, leading them sideways. "The bed's a bit too personal, don't you think?"

He couldn't think. She had him so fired up, he'd settle for the kitchen floor if it would make her happy.

"Here—" She stopped in front of a monstrous reclining apparatus that looked like an adjustable bed in the partially upright position. "The chaise seems more in order for an anonymous...encounter."

Every word she uttered shifted her breasts over his chest by a pleasantly torturous fraction.

"Is that what we're doing? Encountering?"

She wriggled her hips against his. "I don't know about you, but I'm encountering something pretty impressive."

"Honey, you ain't seen nothing yet." Tightening his hold around her waist, he lifted her straight off the floor, dragging her body upward along his and displacing a few of her sequins in the process.

He paused when they were eye to eye.

"Do tell, Detective." Lexi eased the knot on his tie and unbuttoned his shirt just enough to slip her hands underneath the fabric.

Her touch sent him reeling in a way no street-fight punch ever had. Her little hum of approval made him want to protect and serve her all night long.

"I'm not telling you anything, Lexi. You're just going to have to see for yourself." He set her down on the oversize chaise longue and sprawled out alongside her. "Besides, didn't we say anonymous sex meant no talking?"

"No talking?" She looked appalled, but a devilish light in her eyes told him otherwise. "But then, how could I tell you things like this…?"

She leaned close to him, brushing her breast across his upper arm as she cupped her hand around his ear. Her breathy words were soft and warm.

"I want to lick every impressive inch of you."

5

LEXI GUESSED HER WORDS had the desired effect when a ragged groan ripped through the bedroom loud enough to set off her dogs' barking down the hall.

She couldn't help but smile. She felt less like a houseplant every second she passed in Josh's company.

"Still think we ought to impose that 'no talking' rule?" she prompted, sliding his tie out from under his collar and shivering at the sheer sensuality of the sound.

"Did I mention I'm a big proponent of free speech?" Josh flicked one strap of her gown off her shoulder. "I think you ought to feel free to say whatever comes to mind."

Josh's gaze did more than undress her. Somehow, those gray eyes invited her to share her secrets and dared her to bare her soul.

A risk she'd never afforded herself—not with anyone. Nearly two years had passed since her last one-night stand—a blur of awkwardness that hadn't aroused her half as much as Josh's single touch.

No way would she allow their impersonal sex plan to slip off course. She wanted the lights off, blinds down. And all those too-tempting personal glimpses of Josh properly concealed, so she could enjoy her stolen evening revealing other parts of him.

"Say whatever I want? In that case, how about closing those blinds and then I won't hold anything back."

"Whatever the lady wants." Josh moved away from her, taking his searing gaze and his body heat with him.

Lexi watched him prowl about her bedroom, his feral grace not totally out of place in her room full of leopard-print pillows and tiger-striped sheets. Not that he would ever discover those sheets, because she drew the line at letting a stranger sleep in her bed.

Better to have a tryst in the comfort of the chaise longue.

The soft *snap* of the Venetian blinds sliding into place called her from her thoughts. She had a two-second view of Josh by the window before the room was plunged into total darkness. Not even the streetlights penetrated the custom room-darkening shades.

"Better?" His voice loomed closer than she would have expected.

Her heart picked up its pace. A shiver rippled over her skin.

"Better." She wasn't about to admit there was something highly erotic about not being able to see him.

"Good." The low rumble of his voice came from two inches behind her, lifting the hairs on her neck.

"You move pretty fast for a man in strange terrain, Winger."

The chaise cushions shifted as he joined her on the lounger.

"Want me to slow down?" The words whispered over her shoulder seconds before his lips touched her skin there.

Warm, soft, deceptively lazy.

Lexi suspected this man was as ready as she felt inside. Yet he lingered, his kiss thorough and deliberate.

"Slow is good," she admitted. She didn't realize she was edging back toward the hard length of his body until her sequins snagged one of his shirt buttons.

The absolute dark hid him from her, made her feel free to be bold. She reached backward to palm his thigh, running her fingertips over the lightweight gabardine of his trousers.

She hadn't thought it possible for the man to be any harder, but his whole body took one more step toward petrifaction beneath her questing hands. He imprisoned her wrist before she could fully explore the effects of her touch.

He hissed out a breath between his teeth. "Do you ever sit still?" he asked, tugging aside the veil of her hair from her back.

It wasn't the first time she'd been asked that particular question, but the way Josh said it made her perpetual motion sound more like a blessing and less like a curse.

Or maybe she was just in a receptive state of mind, given that he was licking a circuitous path between her shoulder blades.

"Sometimes." She found it difficult to concentrate on his question as he started sliding her zipper down her back. "But only if you make it worth my while."

"Are you challenging me?"

"Definitely."

He edged the material of her dress away from her skin, held to her body by a lone shoulder strap. Her back exposed to Josh's touch but not his gaze, Lexi waited breathlessly for that first caress.

"I wouldn't want to disappoint you."

He breathed the words over her spine, surprising her with the proximity of his mouth and not his hands.

She trembled, anticipating his kiss.

Finally, his lips brushed over her spine between her shoulders, a fluttery kiss that teased more than it satisfied. Heat spiraled through her, flooding her limbs and pooling in her belly.

She moved to turn and face him, to wrest what she needed from him, but he held her hips in place with his hands.

"Wait." He pulled her back against him, allowed her to feel the spectacular length of his body again. His mouth hovered near her ear, mingled in her hair. "Wait one more minute and then I promise I will make you want to be absolutely still."

His hand dipped into her dress, cupping the curve of her hip and skimming the satin of her panties for one heart-stopping minute before he traced a slow path up her spine with his fingers.

Lexi decided she could wait. She could definitely wait.

"I want to at least see you with my hands." Josh

explored the curve of her waist, the soft skin under her arm.

Lexi thought she couldn't be any hungrier for him, until he found the hooks of her strapless bra and popped them free. As her bra slid into the folds of her gaping dress, leaving her breasts bared, she realized she'd been dead wrong.

Slipping the remaining strap of her dress down her shoulder, Josh slid her dress all the way to her feet. Wearing only her panties, she wriggled backward to indulge in the feel of Josh against her naked back.

To find he wasn't there.

"Josh?" Maybe she'd be able to hear him move around the room better if her heart wasn't thundering in her ears.

"Over here." His muffled voice called to her from somewhere in the room near the chaise.

He was obviously standing again. "I think I need to shed at least some of these clothes before I touch you, because I don't think I'm going to be able to stop once I get started."

Her disappointment vanished, transformed to a sense of feminine power.

She reached a hand upward in the darkness, desperate to find him and to ease the longing ache that plagued her. Fingertips moving through the inky blackness, her ears straining to catch any telltale sounds, Lexi yelped when Josh caught her hips and dragged her to the edge of the lounger.

"Can you see me?"

"No."

His voice rumbled above her as he climbed back

onto the lounger. "I can tell when you get close because of your perfume."

His hands slid down her thighs and up the insides of her legs.

"And I can feel your heat." His fingers paused at the juncture of her thighs.

"Oh." She grew very still.

Just as she found his shoulders in the darkness, his lips found her breast and tasted her with a thoroughness that had her panting. He'd ditched his shirt and tie, leaving him clad only in his trousers.

Lexi explored the bare muscle of his chest and shoulders, marveled at the silky texture of the hair on his chest and the well-defined abs just above his waistband.

His smoky whiskey scent mingled with her floral essence, the heat of their bodies intensifying the effect. They fell back into the sea of leopard-print pillows, the faux fur cushioning them as they tumbled onto each other.

Josh's mouth never strayed from her breast. He smoothed his cheek against her nipple, tempting her with the soft rasp of a jaw in need of another shave. He licked a path from one nipple to the other, his fingers playing along whichever one he had left in need.

Lexi wriggled her way on top of him, fitting herself over his erection despite the layers of clothes still between them. Josh groaned his encouragement.

When her hand dipped into the waistband of his pants, however, he flipped her onto her back again.

"That's a risk I'm not willing to take just yet."

"No?" How interesting. She liked thinking her touch was that potent to him.

"No."

He pinned her legs to the chaise with his body. She could tell his head was about level with her abdomen, judging by the way his breath fanned out over her bare belly.

Faux fur caressed her on one side, warm muscle on the other side. A heady combination.

"Ladies first." Josh trailed his finger along the lace edge of her panties. "I'm a gentleman at heart, Lex."

His use of her name called her from her sensual reverie for a moment, reminding her this night was probably getting far too personal, despite their best intentions. How would she ever forget Josh Winger after this?

But then his lips lowered to her navel and she put all thoughts of tomorrow aside. She wouldn't allow herself to miss out on tonight, not when Josh was touching her as she'd never been touched before.

His tongue flicked over her belly and down to her panties, snaking beneath the hem to tease her beyond reason.

She'd never committed the bold act that she suspected Josh was about to. In her world of stringent personal boundaries, that sort of intimacy seemed even greater than straightforward sex.

But tonight didn't follow her rules, and she didn't want it to. Sensual greed had taken hold of her, right about the time she'd first handcuffed herself to this man, and she intended to follow wherever that delicious hunger might lead.

Just as soon as she indulged in one final round of tonight's game of hot pursuit.

JOSH COULDN'T fill his hands with enough of her. Lexi's lithe little body slid around the chaise longue, disappeared into the mountain of pillows, then resurfaced at newly enticing angles.

She wriggled and trembled, shivered and shimmied her way away from him, then sighed and moaned her way back again.

He flung two pillows away and slid her thighs closer to him. By now he was starving for a taste of her.

"Woman, holding you still is like chasing quicksilver."

"Are you having a hard time holding me down, Detective?" she whispered, that throaty voice alone enough to send him over the edge.

"I'm having a hard time all right," he growled. He'd been so careful not to use the wrestling approach on her, but he'd never needed a leg lock so badly.

He heard a jingle a few feet above his head.

"Then, why don't you show me how a real jailer uses these?"

Her words teased him to outer limits of control he hadn't known he possessed. He knew what she was holding in her hands, damn it. He didn't need the light to see those handcuffs in his mind.

"You're kidding." He held himself very still so as

not to snap that taut leash on his restraint. If anyone ought to be wearing cuffs, it was him.

"I assure you, I'm very serious."

Her voice wrapped around him like a seductive devil on his shoulder, the voice of everything wicked he'd ever wanted to do. "You don't know me well enough to let me do that."

Damn but it was hard listening to the good half of his conscience.

"I saw your badge with my own eyes. Besides, they're not real. I could free myself if I really wanted to...although I have the feeling I won't."

The smile in her voice was obvious. She jingled the cuffs above him.

She was enjoying every minute of his torment.

So much for adopting the good cop act tonight. That had never been his style, anyhow.

"You're playing with fire, Lexi." Following the jingling sound, he snatched the cuffs unerringly out of her grip.

"Don't I know it." She shifted her thighs underneath him, moved her body restlessly against his. "I'm loving every minute of it."

Her words chased away any hesitation in Josh. If the lady wanted to play, who was he to spoil her fantasies?

He located one of her fidgety arms and smoothed his hand up and down its silky length. She was toned and trim, supple but delicate to the touch.

On his final sweep down the length of her arm, he slowed his touch to gently massage the skin around her wrist. With his thumb he located her leaping pulse and soothed the throbbing vein.

She practically purred at his ministrations, her whole body humming with contented sighs.

Until he tapped one cuff into place around her wrist.

Her breath caught on a gasp and then released in a slow hiss between her teeth.

He waited, gauged her reaction, weighed her response.

Soon, she flaunted her free hand by walking her fingers right up the middle of his chest.

"Not so fast, sister." He captured the free hand and chained it to its partner. "You're not the one calling the shots here."

The sound of her breathing dominated the dark room, coming in quick, shallow pants.

"No?"

The quiver of excitement in her voice ignited his desire, robbed him of the last shreds of his self-control. "Definitely not." He proved the point by looping her arms over her head to rest on a hill of pillows.

Finally, she remained where he had put her.

Naked but for a scrap of soft satin, Lexi lay before him handcuffed and breathless, yet because of the anonymous sex rule, Josh couldn't witness any of it with his eyes.

He vowed then and there to recreate this scenario one day when he could have the pleasure of seeing it.

For now, his imagination did a credible job of providing him with visuals, while he counted himself lucky to be here with wild-woman Lexi at all.

"So how does it feel to fall from mighty jailer status to helpless captivity in the course of an evening?" He eased away from her to shove off the rest of his clothes. The next time he touched her, nothing would hold him back.

"Don't be so sure of yourself, sweet lips," she purred back. "I could turn the tables at any moment and make you my love slave—no matter how many chains you clamp around me."

"That's pretty big talk considering your utter defenselessness, don't you think?" He yanked a condom out of his wallet and cursed the fact he only carried around one. He'd be damn sure to use it wisely.

"I dare you to come closer and say that, Detective."

Heat practically radiated from her in waves. Josh could feel her sultry warmth, sense the position of her body even in the dark as he leaned over the chaise once again.

Her exotic scent filled his nostrils. Flowers and musk—hothouse sex.

She moved to loop her handcuffed wrists around his head, but he was having none of it. Before her arms could settle around his neck, he secured her wrists above her head with one hand and lay his other palm over the front of her panties.

Her body shuddered, shivered, lifted off the chaise

to meet his touch. He kissed away her hungry whimper, rubbed away the chill bumps on her thighs with his fingers.

"Are you ready for me yet?" he whispered into the tangled silken mass of her hair. Her ear lay below those spiral curls somewhere.

His finger skimmed up the inside of her thigh, stopping just short of her satin panties.

Her moaned affirmative was part womanly plea, part threatening snarl.

He found her slick with desire and deliciously ready. The scrap of satin didn't stand a chance against her heat and his hunger. With a snap of his wrist, he snagged them straight off her hips, shredding the seams in a noisy ripping of fabric.

Lexi made a little squeal of delight and wrapped one of her legs around his.

Unwilling to be distracted, Josh maneuvered his shoulders beneath her thighs, positioning her body for the kiss he'd wanted to give her ever since she'd slithered her way out of her black sequins.

She tasted like rich red wine, and she clouded his senses twice as fast. He would have indulged in her all night, but too soon her thighs went taut, her hips flexing upward off the lounger.

The shriek that should have accompanied her orgasm must have been released into the stuffing of one of her soft velvet pillows, but the muffled cries still reached his ears. Satisfied his male ego. Made him want to bring her to that mind-blowing point all over again.

"Please," she finally managed to say between deep, gasping breaths.

The cuffs jingled in completion of her thoughts.

He didn't need to ask where the keys were. Josh had seen her work the fake cuffs at the fund-raiser. With the press of a button, the links fell open, freeing Lexi and unleashing a small-scale attack.

She fell on him, rolling him onto his back sideways across the chaise.

"You are so all mine now, Winger."

6

THE EARTH HAD MOVED.

Lexi still shook from the tremors of the most incredible orgasm ever—not that she'd had many for comparison's sake. But she knew from the way her body trembled inside and out that she'd just experienced majorly amazing sex by anyone's standards.

And they hadn't even done *it* yet.

She meant to remedy that situation right now.

"I want you." Whispering the words in Josh's ear, Lexi wriggled over his body, savoring every provocative sensation the man inspired. "Now."

"There's a condom on the floor near my pants." He molded her hips with his hands, measured her waist with his fingers, spanned her belly with his palms.

Lexi hadn't even thought about protection. She had no intention of getting personal with Josh Winger, but she had to admit, he was the kind of man a woman could trust to protect her in every possible way.

Searching over her bedroom carpet with her hands, Lexi found the packet and handed it to him.

A snicker of satisfaction rolled through her when she thought about the stud on the condom-dispensing machine she'd seen in the women's restroom earlier tonight.

Josh was ten times the stud that man was. And she'd snagged him.

Josh handed the condom back to her, and the packet brushed her fingers in the darkness. "Will you?"

Not a simple request for a woman who had never put a condom on a man before. Lexi's snicker faded.

"I'm no good with those things."

She could hear the condom packet ripping open and Josh rolling on the device without her aid.

"I hope you mean the condom and not what's inside."

"I'm very good with what's inside." She hoped. She wanted to be. After that orgasm he'd given her, Lexi wanted him to see stars. Solar systems, maybe.

Luckily, the impersonal dark gave her the brashness to straddle him. She never would have been able to carry off tonight's sexy scenarios with the lights on, but the utter blackness of the room gave her permission to be daring. The darkness gave her confidence a boost, removed all insecurities about her appearance, making her feel beautiful.

Taking what she wanted most, Lexi guided his rigid length inside her by slow degrees.

He filled her so completely, stretched her so lusciously. Her world narrowed to the hot, seductive sensations he imparted.

She tested the length of him, easing herself away from him until he nearly withdrew, then edging back down to join them together fully. Lost in her enjoyment of a body that brought her so much pleasure, Lexi was surprised when he flipped her to lay on her back again.

His chest seemed to surround her in a wall of fur-covered muscle. She couldn't see him—but everywhere she reached, she felt him. Soft velvet hair over steely sinew.

She wanted to remain there, wrapped in the safe, sexy haven of his powerful body, but he reached between her thighs to touch her again.

That unerring thumb found the source of all her pleasure and gently plucked. Sensual satisfaction pulsed through her like electric waves. Lexi would have lost it again—if he hadn't nearly withdrawn for a moment.

She lingered on the brink, her body coiled with pleasure, until he slid back inside her and sent her hurtling headlong into the sultry abyss. His groan of fulfillment comforted her, assured her she wasn't the only one flying apart in the haven of a chaise longue tonight.

As aftershocks rippled through them, Lexi marveled that a certain dangerous detective had lost his cool right along with her, and it couldn't have been more satisfying, more rewarding, or more terrifying.

Lexi had allowed herself to be far more personal with Josh than with any other man she'd slept with. If she wasn't careful, she'd find herself caring about him—about what he thought, about whether or not he liked her in return.

And she wouldn't allow that. Not when she'd

fought for so long not to care what anyone thought of her.

All she had to do was make sure he left before dawn. Then maybe she could pretend this had all been a regular one-night stand, instead of something earth shattering.

But the heat of his body was mesmerizing now, and dawn was blessedly hours away. She snuggled closer to his shoulder, reveling in yet another heady experience she'd always missed out on—wrapping herself around a man's body and cuddling into the crook of his arm.

She could afford herself a few more hours with Josh, a little more time to enjoy their over-the-top chemistry. Just as long as he was out of her bed by morning.

Because no matter how many hair-curling orgasms Josh Winger had the power to give her, Lexi wasn't about to allow their relationship to turn into something personal.

Handcuffs she could handle, but sharing her toothpaste was a risk she had no intention of taking.

JOSH WOKE to the soft whimper of a dog.

He didn't need to pry his eyes open to remember precisely where he was and why. Lexi's perfume had scented all his dreams, while her wild hair had been his only blanket. But the cop in him had no choice but to investigate the canine problem.

Sunlight had managed to permeate the blinds, providing him with his first glimpse of the bedroom he'd slept in—or rather, the apartment's jungle headquarters.

Tiger stripes decorated half the pillows on the chaise, while some sort of cheetah or leopard print covered the rest. Everything was faux fur or velvet, including the black lounger.

A few feet away, a mammoth bed dominated the room, its pristine white linen coverings protected by a suspended tent of floor-length mosquito netting. Any wooden furniture was dark mahogany—the headboard, a bookshelf, a nightstand—and all of it showcased elaborate carvings.

But the furniture and framed prints of exotic animals weren't what held his attention. It was the walls covered with framed photos that accomplished that feat.

There was silence from the whimpering dog for a few moments, while Josh let his eyes roam the pictures of Lexi in her charitable mode. Some photos were from glitzy events like last night's fund-raiser; in each one Lexi was dressed to the nines. In a few, she had her arm slung around well-known actors and actresses; in others, she embraced pint-size kids sporting ball caps that only partially hid the effects of chemotherapy.

There was obviously a lot more to this woman than he'd realized. More heart. More generosity. He touched a photo of Lexi riding on the back of someone's wheelchair at the Special Olympics. Lexi tangoing with a woman bearing a shirt that read "I'm a Survivor." Both women wore the pink ribbons that raised awareness for breast cancer.

He still couldn't shake the feeling that he'd seen Lexi somewhere before tonight. Maybe he'd been at one of these events? No. How could he ever have seen a woman like her and not remember?

Josh was squinting to see the details of a photo showing Lexi in a soup kitchen wearing an oversize red T-shirt with a Christmas tree on it, when the sound of the canine whimper distracted him.

He snuck a glance at Lexi, but she didn't appear to hear. Last night's dominatrix now had an innocent face, a mouth hanging half open in sleep, and a blanket of black hair covering a shapely naked body.

When the whine came again, Josh remembered Lexi's menagerie greeting them at the door last night. If that brood was still stuffed in the guest bedroom, they would definitely be crying by now.

Wide awake now, Josh slid off the lounger and located his pants, all the while wondering what the protocol should be for the morning after a night of anonymous sex.

Logic said he should just slip out the door. She was the one who'd wanted it to be impersonal, right?

Josh slid into his pants and zipped up, then padded his way into the hallway. The other women he knew never minded him leaving without a big goodbye. But then, those women were as likely to be his beer-drinking buddies, sparring partners or weightlifting spotters.

Those women couldn't be more different from the femme fatale he'd spent the night with.

Locating the front door in the living room, Josh oriented himself. Guessing the guest bedroom was the other closed door off the living area, he turned the knob.

And found himself floored by a pack of wild dogs.

"Hey!" Flat on his back, he shouted at the horde of mutts in his scariest bad cop voice, but the canine crew didn't stand down. They licked his cheeks and sniffed where they had no damn business. The littlest one, a fur ball with no discernable eyes, climbed right on his chest and pranced around excitedly in circles.

"Mush." He brushed off his limited knowledge of dog language to reestablish command of the situation. "Heel." The dogs worked together to keep him on the living room floor, on his back. They ran around him in such tight circles that he didn't have any room to move. "Will you sit down, damn it?"

They seemed to recognize something in that sentence. Josh made a mental note that they must respond to either curse words or "sit" commands.

"That's better." He hauled himself up to his feet as the pack of dogs watched him with wide eyes. Except for the fur ball, who probably couldn't see past the pink bow falling down over her forehead.

"Only three of you?" Where had the other ten dogs disappeared? "How is it three little mutts make as much racket as a kennel full of normal-size dogs?"

Before they could answer, Josh's pants began to ring.

He fished in his back pocket for his cell phone, before it woke Lexi.

"Winger."

"I'm on my way out the door, Columbo," Josh's partner, Duke Rawlins began without prelude. "Unless you tell me you have a hot lead that forces me to stay in town this weekend.''

"As if I'd give Amanda any reason to kick my ass." Josh plunked down into a wide white chair in the shape of a scalloped seashell. Where the bedroom had been the jungle, the living room seemed to be the sea. Aqua-colored walls and lamps made of pink coral provided color for a room furnished all in white.

"Yeah, me either. Forget I asked." Duke laughed the goofy guy-in-love laugh. He'd always been the "good cop" half of their partnership, but ever since he'd fallen for Amanda Matthews, he had added "sappy, would-be family guy" to the list of his good traits.

"Seriously, I just wanted to find out if you learned anything new last night."

That Duke had to call and ask him was more of a wakeup call than the dogs barking this morning. Josh sure as hell had gotten sidetracked last night if he'd managed to forget all about the smugglers he had been following for two months.

"My cover was blown early on. I didn't get a chance to look into a damn thing."

A sudden round of yapping from the doggie set gave Josh the perfect excuse not to explain himself. He definitely didn't relish the idea of telling Duke how on his big undercover mission he'd wound up handcuffed and sitting in a fake jail cell half the night.

"I'm in control, though," he shouted over the dogs as he turned to see what they were barking about.

"I'll tell you all about it when I—" He forgot what he'd been about to say when Lexi strolled into the room wearing a long red silk robe with—honest to God—a little train of material trailing behind her.

She cocked a hip to one side. "Don't let me stop you. Go ahead. Tell him all about it now."

"I'll catch up with you next week, bud. Gotta go." Josh slapped the phone closed, well aware from Lexi's haughty pose that he'd probably done something wrong already. "Morning."

"Yes, it is." She agreed with him a bit too wholeheartedly.

"You were hoping I'd have vacated the premises by now, weren't you." No use dancing around the issue. He'd made the wrong decision by staying past dawn. A pity, considering he'd been hoping to leave on a peaceful "I'll call you" sort of note.

Was it such a crime that he'd entertained the notion of seeing her again? Sure, she was like a walking scattergun to his well-focused world. But that didn't mean he couldn't at least have a cup of coffee with her after everything they'd shared.

Besides, he was so close to remembering how he knew her. His smuggling investigation might be headed down the toilet, but he could at least solve the mystery of why Lexi looked so damn familiar....

LEXI SHIVERED under Josh's assessing stare. Did she expect him to be gone this morning? Sort of like she expected the *New York Times* to be on her welcome mat.

Of course she did.

"Anonymous sex sounds like something that should have circumvented an awkward morning-after, doesn't it?'' She sounded like a serious bitch. And the red robe she'd yanked out of her closet surely only added to the image.

But if she didn't start drawing boundaries fast, Josh would see beyond her daring facade to the houseplant underneath. She needed to keep her public face very separate from the private one if she wanted to survive in her business. Josh wouldn't want to know the Lexi whose idea of excitement on a Saturday was taking her dogs for a walk.

Josh patted her miniature poodle absently on the head as he stared at Lexi.

''Sorry about that.'' His big, tanned hands moved awkwardly around Muffin's ears as he re-tied the pink bow falling out of her fur. ''It just didn't feel right to run out of here this morning without saying goodbye.''

Lexi's bitch imitation couldn't withstand the appeal of a man who could groom a poodle without feeling like his *machismo* had been compromised.

''You want some breakfast?'' She had to at least ask.

''That's okay. I'm just going to grab my jacket.'' He jerked a thumb toward her bedroom, and she nodded.

He came back in moments, buttoning his shirt. ''I don't look familiar to you by any chance, do I?''

Familiar from her fantasies, maybe. He was everything Lexi wanted in a fantasy man, just a little too dangerous for the real world.

Still, Lexi wanted to pull him back to her bedroom and beg for a replay of last night—this time with lights on so she could watch him touch her body in glorious, living color.

"No," she managed finally. "Should you?"

"I keep thinking I've seen you somewhere before."

"I don't think so." She could feel his eyes on her as she bent to pick up Muffin. No doubt her dog felt very neglected after Lexi snubbed her last night in favor of Josh. She could only hope Muffin's feminine eye would take one look at the detective and understand Lexi's decision.

Scooping up the dog, Lexi walked toward the door, needing to bid goodbye to Josh before she did something stupid, like invite him to watch *The View* or help her with the Sunday crossword. Yeah, he'd be pretty wowed by last night's bad girl then.

"Guess that's my cue to head out." Josh followed her through the living room to the front door. "But I can't regret not sneaking out like a thief in the night, Lexi. I had a really good time."

Blush.

Double blush.

Of course he had a great time. She'd demanded they play bondage games in the dark. She had a pretty good idea what men thought about women who acted like that on the first date.

"Um. Me, too." Social awkwardness didn't scale any greater heights, but Lexi refused to cringe. She opted to open the door and wave Muffin's paw at him. "'Bye, Josh."

He didn't move. Not even an eyelash. He watched her with light gray eyes frozen in place.

"Holy hell, I know exactly who you are."

Great, he already had her pegged for a closet houseplant? He took a step back, a horrified look on his face.

"And it's that bad?" She'd go to the mat that he'd had a good time last night. How disappointed could he be in who she was?

"I knew I remembered you from somewhere. Seeing you holding the dog just made it all come crashing back to me. You're Amanda Matthews's best friend." He slapped his forehead with enough force to jar the diamond stud in his ear. "You might as damn well be Duke's sister-in-law, for that matter."

"You know Amanda?" Lexi set down her dog, a sinking feeling telling her Josh had just somehow penetrated her inner circle of friends.

All three of her dogs milled about their mistress, sensing trouble.

"I'm Duke's partner. You probably don't remember seeing me the day I came into Amanda's shop to investigate a drug smuggling case, but you and I passed each other in the doorway once."

No. She shook her head, willing away the connection with the man who she needed to remain anonymous. "Ohmigod. *You're* Columbo?"

Normally, Lexi would have been flattered that Josh remembered her months later. She did sort of remember seeing a dangerous-looking guy with Duke once, before they'd been formally introduced.

But Lexi could hardly savor the compliment of Josh remembering her. Not when their relationship had just shifted from a one-night stand to something about as far from impersonal as two people could possibly get. Their best friends were getting married, for crying out loud. With the way her luck was running, they'd likely be stuck pulling best man and maid of honor duties together.

So much for anonymous sex. She and Josh might as well still be handcuffed together, because they no longer stood a chance in hell of walking away from last night.

HE WAS SO DEAD.

A few hours after he'd left Lexi's, Josh pumped quarters into a newspaper vending machine on the corner of Sixth Avenue and West Twentieth Street. Damn, but he'd like to spend his last weeks among the living. When Duke returned from his motorcycle trip, he was going to pound Josh for sleeping with Amanda's best friend.

Ever since Duke had fallen for Amanda, he seemed to have forgotten one-night stands were part of dating. Duke had turned as stand-up damn honorable as his John Wayne namesake, and he would probably fail to see the fun in Josh handcuffing Amanda's best friend.

He slid a copy of the *Daily News* from the box and stuffed it under his arm as he trekked toward the Tenth Precinct.

Lexi hadn't wasted any time giving him the boot after they'd figured out their unwanted connection. She'd been polite enough about it, but Josh knew she was stressed by the way she clutched her poor shih tzu to her chest as she concocted lame excuses about not being able to see him again.

What made her so adamant about not getting personal with him? He weighed the situation as he wove around a few cop cars outside the station, exchanging greetings with a handful of beat cops headed out for their day on the streets.

He'd never minded when women from his gym had come on to him for a one-night stand, but it bugged him to think that's all Lexi wanted from him.

Not that *he* necessarily wanted anything more. Lexi was a limelight girl and he was an undercover kind of guy. Josh had the feeling she would be a walking explosion to his well-ordered world.

And what made it worse was that she was tight with Amanda and Duke. Any cop worth his salt would have figured out who Lexi was during the two hours he'd spent locked in a jail cell last night. Why hadn't he seen it? He'd known Amanda's best friend was some sort of fashion journalist who spent half her time abroad covering runway shows.

But he'd been so caught up thinking about Lexi as his personal stalker that he'd missed the bigger picture. Too busy indulging personal fantasies to see what was right in front of his face.

Duke was such an old-fashioned guy that he'd probably pull out some pithy wisdom about why Josh shouldn't expect to get his milk for free. And even if Duke managed to get past it, if Lexi ever said anything about the encounter that upset Amanda, Josh would not only be dead, but mutilated first. Duke allowed nothing, but nothing, to upset his princess.

Shit.

Josh tugged open the precinct door and glowered

his way down the hall. His phone was ringing when he sat down at his desk. Instinct told him to ignore it. Professional training wouldn't allow it.

He tossed the newspaper on the desk and sank into his squeaky office chair.

"Winger." He stared up at his framed photo of Rocky Marciano and prayed for some focus.

"I'm in Seaside Heights, New Jersey," the familiar voice of his partner shouted over a crashing surf on the other end. "Ever been down south this far?"

Duke. Just the person Josh didn't want to hear from twice in one morning. He palmed his forehead and squeezed to ease the tension in his temples.

"I've seen enough of Jersey to last me a lifetime." Josh reached for the dumbbell on top of his file cabinet and launched into mindless curls as he talked.

"Not like this, you haven't." Duke covered the mouthpiece and whispered something to his companion, then laughed. No doubt, he and Amanda were having a great time. "I've only got a few minutes, but I wanted to ask a favor."

"Shoot." Maybe Josh could offset his misdeeds with Lexi by lending Duke a hand.

"I was too distracted yesterday when I was tuning up the bike for the trip to really concentrate on what Amanda was saying about her friend getting blasted in her own magazine. But it turns out this friend— Lexi Mansfield—was slammed in print by Simone Bertrand."

Josh set down the dumbbell. "Bertrand is a name on the list of potential smugglers located outside the Garment District."

"Bertrand's also two cards short a deck and strikes me as way too flighty to be a suspect. Given that she's on the list and blasting negative press on Amanda's buddy, however, maybe you could check her out this week and touch base with Lexi?"

"Touch base with Lexi Mansfield." Last time Josh had touched Lexi, she'd felt very fine. Duke was definitely going to kill him. "No problem."

"Excellent—" Duke rattled off Lexi's address and phone number for Josh to copy down—not that Josh needed it.

"Lexi means a lot to Amanda. I want to make damn sure nothing happens to her. Besides, maybe you can at least cross this Bertrand woman off our list."

"I'll follow up today." Even if it meant Lexi would toss him out on his ear, he would at least check on her after he talked to her detractor. He had as much reason as Duke to want to protect Lexi.

Maybe a part of him was glad to have an excuse to see her again—even though it would mean trouble for them both.

"Knew I could count on you. I'm outta here." Duke slammed down the receiver, leaving Josh to wade through the smuggling case on his own.

They'd been working with a special task force for months, and had already nailed one guy and a few of his cohorts for hiding drugs in crates of imported fabric, but the flow of contraband to the Garment District hadn't stopped.

Somehow, drugs were still entering the city under

Josh's watch, and he damn well was going to figure out how. If that meant he'd have to cross Lexi Mansfield's line in the sand, then so be it.

Like it or not, things were about to get personal.

7

SHE WAS IN over her head.

Lexi clicked her way around her apartment in outrageously high heels, hurrying to get dressed and trying not to think about how she'd made a big mistake by sleeping with Josh the night before. Sure, he'd been everything a woman could want between the sheets—or among the velvet pillows, in this case—but he was proving to be pretty damn dangerous to her mental well-being outside the bedroom.

She couldn't stop thinking about him. About his big hands threading through her hair. About the way he'd followed her rules of anonymous sex last night, even though he gladly would have made love with the lights on and their gazes connected.

She slid a tawny-colored evening dress out of her closet, not giving a fig that it was only mid-day. She lived by her own rules, damn it.

Yanking the zipper up her back, she went over the night in her mind, wondering how she could have handled things differently. She might have stood a fighting chance of putting sexy Detective Winger out of her mind if he'd at least been the total stranger she'd first assumed. But she was guaranteed to see him again if he was Duke's partner.

How could she ever look him in the eye in a social setting after everything they'd shared last night?

Her body still quivered just thinking about it. Her legs still ached from wrapping around him so tightly. Her lips were full and swollen from his kisses. All this, and the man had left five hours ago.

She was definitely in over her head.

Maybe that's why she felt compelled to don her highest heels, drape herself in Armani, and scout out Simone Bertrand. Lexi was spoiling for a confrontation, a chance to take control of her life again.

She'd spent the past ten years telling herself she didn't need anyone's approval. This afternoon, she'd remind Simone of that fact and recover her professional balance. As for her private life and her night with Josh...she couldn't imagine recovering her balance there anytime soon.

Thankfully, she didn't have to see him again for a couple of weeks. She and Josh would simply stay out of one another's way until Duke and Amanda returned to New York. And even then, who was to say they'd cross paths in the future?

Lexi checked her wallet to be sure she had enough cash for cab fare, then blew kisses at her babies on the way out the door. Muffin and Snowball barked their goodbyes, but Harry—the terrier—contented himself with a more dignified canine nod.

Josh had wanted a dignified goodbye, a voice whispered in the back of her mind as she took the elevator to the first floor and paused to check her mailbox.

Why did the man have to sneak continually into her thoughts? *Broadcast* himself across her thoughts, was more like it. Josh couldn't have made more of a mental impression if he'd announced his presence with a blasted megaphone.

As she spied the handwriting on the lone small envelope in her box, the swirl of her thoughts ceased. Fear niggled the back of her neck, caused her stomach to churn. She didn't need to open the letter to know it would contain another anonymous note, another threat.

Lexi grabbed it out of her box and stuffed it in her purse, too rattled to read it just yet. She could open it in the cab during the considerable drive to Simone's house in Long Island. Then she could panic in private.

After hailing a taxi, Lexi slid into the seat and gave the driver Simone's address. But even after she read the short note—two lines threatening her babies if she didn't quit "running her mouth" in her weekly column—Lexi didn't truly panic.

All she kept thinking was that Josh would be able to kick her note writer's butt from the Hudson to the East River if the guy ever tried anything. That line of thinking *did* make her panic.

Because if there was one thing Lexi had learned in life so far, it was that she had to fight her own battles.

And no sexy interlude with a dangerous cop was going to change that fact.

JOSH PRESSED the redial button on his cell phone to try calling Lexi one more time before he rang Simone Bertrand's doorbell. He stood on the brick walkway outside the behemoth mansion in a ritzy section of

Long Island, willing Lexi to pick up her phone this time.

No such luck. The woman didn't even know his phone number, so it's not like she could be ducking her caller I.D. She was genuinely out for the day.

He hated it that he didn't have the slightest notion where she might be. She'd been ever-present in his mind all damn day, yet evidently she wasn't giving him a second blasted thought.

Didn't she remember the heightened sensuality of last night's utter darkness? The complete awareness they'd had of one another? Josh had been with enough women to know nights like that weren't the norm. Why wasn't Lexi walking around her apartment with her pack of dogs at her heels, slowly replaying every nuance of the previous night in her mind?

Besides, he was supposed to check on her, make sure she was safe. How could he do that if she never answered her phone?

Once her answering machine clicked on, Josh folded up his phone and stuffed it in his pocket. He rang the bell at the Bertrand woman's palatial colonial home and waited.

He might not be able to get his update on Lexi, but at least he'd take care of scratching the Long Island designer off his list of smuggling suspects.

Five minutes later he found himself waiting in a prissy sitting room, surrounded by pink silk armchairs and an army of silver animal statuettes. Idly, he ran his finger over two whales and a coiled snake, a pointer dog ready to hunt and an elephant standing on its hind legs.

Josh peered at his reflection in the elephant's back and straightened the lapels of his jacket. Not only did he look more like a thug than a police officer, but also he was out of his depth here.

Duke might know how to talk to these upper crust folks, but Josh didn't have a clue. Give him a few street crooks to tangle with and he could hold his own. Give him a computer and he could tap his way down a paper trail of clues faster than Duke could polish off a burger. But put him in a situation where he had to talk to the owner of enough silver animals to provide flatware for all of Brooklyn and Josh didn't have a clue.

"Detective?" A throaty feminine voice assailed his ears, made him stand up straighter.

Josh turned to find an overblown blonde with a face perfectly sculpted to match a body only a plastic surgeon could have created. The woman had more lift than a hydraulic jack—on the front end, on the back end, around eyebrows that seemed arched in permanent surprise.

"Josh Winger." He nodded. "Ms. Bertrand?"

She didn't bother to confirm or deny it. A wicked grin split her full lips. "If only I had known my local police station was harboring such gorgeous men as you, Detective, I wouldn't have wasted all those nights salivating over the *Law and Order* guys."

"Nice to meet you." He stuck out his hand, unsure how to respond as she squeezed his palm and didn't let go.

"The pleasure is all mine, I assure you." She batted her eyelashes. "I noticed you admiring my statues. I have a collection of much more *interesting* pieces upstairs if you'd like to come see them."

Sure. Right after he looked at her etchings.

"Actually, Ms. Bertrand—"

"Call me Simone." She squeezed his arm as if to impress the wish upon him.

"Actually, Simone, I was hoping you could talk to me about how your design firm handles its imports."

The flirtatious light in her eyes dimmed a bit. "Imports?"

"Fabrics or any other material you order from abroad."

She assumed a theatrical pout. Josh noticed her lower lip seemed to have the same buoyant lift as the rest of her.

"If I indulge you now, Detective, will you indulge me later?"

Josh realized he wasn't even a little tempted. Not that he would have hit the sheets with a potential suspect in a million years. But usually the purely male side of his brain felt the pull of such an offer.

Not today, when Lexi Mansfield's lithe little body clung to his memories with tenacious blue fingernails.

"Sorry, Ms. Bertrand." He plucked the woman's fingers off his jacket. "I'm afraid I can't return the favor."

The snappy *click* of high heels across the marble corridor floor alerted him to a new arrival. A feminine new arrival.

He'd scarcely had time to turn around before Lexi's voice echoed through the large room.

"Josh?"

The look of betrayal on Lexi's face couldn't have been any more apparent. A beleaguered butler stood at her side as she stopped short in the entryway.

"Ms. Alexandra Mansfield is here, Ms. Bertrand," the butler announced with a mixture of stiff formality and impatience.

"It's Lexi," she snapped, obviously recovering from her moment of undisguised emotion.

Had Josh really seen a flash of jealousy, or was it wishful thinking on his part?

"Not according to your mother, miss," the butler returned, bowing in deferential response to Lexi's mild snarl.

"Honestly, your staff is as ill-mannered as you, Simone. Jeeves should have told me you were busy." Lexi adjusted the shoulder strap of her purse and tossed her long, dark hair over her shoulder.

She looked phenomenal. Her dress clung to her curves without cinching them, the fabric molding around her body like a lover's hand.

"It's James, Ms. Mansfield," the butler called from some distance down the hallway.

Josh hid a laugh, and thought he noticed a smile playing about Lexi's lips, too.

"Yes, I am very busy," Simone responded to Lexi's earlier comment. "You'll have to come back later."

All traces of Lexi's smile disappeared. "You can count on it, Simone. I'll keep Jeeves entertained until you're finished with your—'' Lexi's eyes skated over Josh ''—business.''

Josh became acutely aware that Simone still seemed attached to his arm despite his earlier efforts to free himself. Lexi sure as hell hadn't missed his incriminating position.

Still, she pivoted on her skyscraper heels with the precision of a drill sergeant. Josh couldn't take his eyes off her, as a loose-limbed walk carried her and all that in-your-face attitude out of view.

He gladly would have chased after her if he didn't have to interrogate the vine clinging to his arm.

But at least he could cross one task off his list today. He'd checked on Lexi, as Duke had requested.

And from what he could see, she was fantastic.

Any way he looked at it, Lexi Mansfield was one hell of a woman.

JOSH WINGER was a first-class bastard.

Lexi repeated the sentiment in every language she knew. Thanks to Lexi's frequent trips around the world for her magazine, the exercise took her all the way from Simone's hideous pink parlor to her free-form swimming pool and fussy gardens in the backyard.

Unfortunately, it didn't ease the sting of seeing the man she was struggling to forget, in the clutches of her socially mortal enemy. How did Josh know Simone?

Worse yet, why was Lexi sticking around to find out?

Even as she asked herself the question, Lexi knew

the answer. She liked Josh. And in spite of her best efforts not to complicate her life with relationships that could only hurt her, Lexi found herself wanting to do just that.

She took a seat in a cast-iron garden chair next to a small table, determined to talk to Simone sometime today. She just hoped it wasn't tomorrow morning before the woman finished her business.

The thought make Lexi's stomach churn.

But maybe it was just as well she'd discovered Josh had other women in his life. Maybe this would be the immunization shot she needed to resist him.

She released a long-suffering sigh, not realizing she wasn't alone until she heard the slam of a silver tray on the table beside her.

"Rough day, miss?" James Preston, the Bertrand's longtime butler, asked politely.

Lexi glared at him for good measure, but she'd always secretly liked the uptight gentleman her father had once hired as her elocution tutor when she was in high school.

She'd grown up two blocks from here, a social misfit with her academic parents. The Mansfields had been well-off by most of the world's standards, but peasants by this neighborhood's standards.

Simone had thrived on teasing Lexi since their shared days at a posh boarding school in the city, but she'd gone too far with her letter to Lexi's editor.

"Gawd-awful," Lexi responded in her best New Jersey accent, just to torment him. "I see Her Majesty is holding court today?"

James sat down beside her and poured them both

a cup of tea from his silver tray. He might be the butler, but he was the Bertrand household's only claim to refinement, and he ruled the roost in a way Simone never could.

"The gentleman is a New York police detective," James confided. "I hope Simone hasn't gotten herself into any trouble."

"Nothing she can't handle with her ten-thousand-dollar body, I'm sure."

James seemed to battle a grin as he passed her a cup of tea with a half lemon. "I'll admit she loves to make trouble, but this marks our first visit from the authorities."

"I don't suppose they can arrest her for disparaging my character in a public forum, can they?" Lexi sipped her tea, soothed by both the companionship and the drink.

"Her letter was disgraceful. I'd like to go on record as having recommended against that course of action."

"Thank you. It did seem a bit over the top, even for Simone."

James looked as if he would comment further, but after a fierce frown, he suddenly changed the topic.

"Is there any chance you can wrangle me an invitation to the Dance for Children ball next month?"

"No offense, James, but its five hundred dollars a plate. Are you sure you want to go?"

"Maria's niece was diagnosed with leukemia this year, and we wanted to make a contribution. I thought this would be a nice way to do it, if it's not too much trouble."

Lexi wondered if Simone would shell out half as much money to the Dance for Children as her big-hearted butler.

"Done. Tell Maria I'm sorry to hear about her niece and I'll call her this week. Maybe we can run something in my column on this."

"Thank you." James finished his tea and replaced his cup on the platter. "If you are not careful, my dear, you are going to turn into the grand dame of New York's social scene before you know it."

"I'll leave that to Simone. You know I pride myself on being a loose cannon in the social realm."

"Yes, but you have the much-needed attribute of a generous spirit."

He stood to leave, but before Lexi could protest, Simone's brother, Anton, rounded the corner of the house.

The male counterpart of Simone's blond perfection, Anton was not only handsome, but also reasonably nice. He'd occasionally stepped in to staunch Simone's mouth when no one else had been able to, and his kindness had saved Lexi from more than a few playground scrapes.

"Lexi!" Anton kissed her on both cheeks, his white sweater and gym bag suggesting he'd been at the tennis courts. "What a nice surprise. I should have known when James didn't answer the door that you were around here somewhere. You seem to be the only person who can distract the old man."

He gave James a playful punch to the arm, but the dignified butler merely walked away with his tea tray.

"Good luck, Ms. Alexandra," he called.

"Thanks, Jeeves." She kept a wary eye on Anton as he pulled James's vacated chair as close to Lexi as possible.

"I am so sorry about Simone's recent nastiness." He reached for Lexi's hands.

"I'll set her straight." She reached to fix her hair, not wanting to hear Anton's apologies for his sister. The two of them were as dysfunctional and co-dependent as ever. Their parents had died two years ago, leaving them more money than either of them was really mature enough to handle.

Lexi kept her eyes trained over Anton's shoulder for signs of Josh. She kept hoping he'd leave the house soon, so she could tell herself he wasn't really sleeping with Simone.

"Let me talk to my sister, Lexi," Anton volunteered. "You've probably had enough to deal with in the fallout of this mess. You don't need to listen to Simone's put-downs, too."

"Thanks, but I think I need to talk to her myself." Lexi hated to admit she'd been spoiling for a fight all day, when Anton obviously wanted to play chivalrous savior.

She thought she heard a door slam somewhere inside the house, and squinted across the side yard to where the plain black Ford was parked. She had an idea that would be Josh's car, probably a police vehicle.

Anton seized her hands while she wasn't looking. "No, Lexi. I insist." He cupped her chin in his hand. "I want to make this right for you. Let me take care of it."

From nowhere, Josh Winger appeared between them, his big shadow falling across Anton in more ways than one.

Anton let go of her instantly.

"Too late," Josh informed him, his words clipped. "I already took care of it."

A little thrill passed through Lexi. Not because she needed Josh taking care of her, but because Josh had already finished up with Simone and come looking for Lexi.

Her mood improved just a little.

"Come on." Josh tugged Lexi's arm. "Let's go."

"I'm not going anywhere until I speak to Simone." Lexi ignored the electric shock of his touch, the leap of every nerve ending through the sheer fabric around her arms.

Josh didn't respond right away. He was still looking in Anton's direction, his face twisted into an expression Lexi could have read from fifty yards away.

She'd never seen anyone communicate "get lost" quite so effectively.

"We'll catch up with each other soon, Lexi." Anton grabbed his gym bag and backed toward the house. "Nice to see you."

He all but ran the last few steps. No wonder, considering Josh looked like he'd just walked off *The Godfather* set with his dark hair and heavy eyebrows, his prominent scar gracing one cheek.

If Lexi had any sense, she'd be running, too. Though, of course, for entirely different reasons.

"Isn't that police intimidation or something?" Lexi asked mildly, studying her nails.

Josh had her hauled out of her seat and onto her feet in seconds. It happened so fast, she barely had time to react, but her treacherous body had followed his command on instinct.

"We need to get out of here." His words were a husky whisper, not unlike the voice he'd used in the bedroom last night....

"I need to talk to Simone, Josh, and I'm not leaving until I do." She reminded herself about taking control of her life again. "You are breaking all the rules of an anonymous encounter by following me around today."

That caught his attention. His eyes widened.

"Who's following who, lady? I was here first, remember?"

"And you're free to leave first, too. I'm an independent woman, remember?" She folded her arms across herself in staunch defense. "I don't need you, Winger."

His jaw worked that over for a long moment.

He looked damn good in his black jacket and dark T-shirt underneath. He definitely looked like a bad ass. What turned her on even more was the fact that he probably *was* a bad ass. A fact even Mr. Knight in Shining Armor Anton had been wise to in the space of three seconds.

"Then here's a newsflash for you, Ms. Independent." He glowered at her with his light gray eyes, leaning just a little too close. "I happen to need *you.*"

Her heart jumped at the notion.

Lexi chided it, told herself she'd imagined the reaction. "Are you intimating something sexual?"

"No, I'm not intimating something sexual. I want to keep my teeth, thank you." The barest hint of a grin played at his lips. "I need your fashion world knowledge, not your body. But if you're offering—"

"Don't ruin it, Winger." She plucked her purse off the ground where she'd dropped it during her impromptu cup of tea with James, then looped the strap over her shoulder. She didn't need his brand of temptation right now—not when she'd been warding off thoughts of him all day. "If it's fashion you need to know about, you've obviously come to the right woman."

"You'll come with me now? Back to the city?"

Lexi noticed he didn't try to pull her along anymore. He was letting *her* make the call as to whether she went with him or not. She really needed to talk to Simone, but curiosity about what Josh wanted was eating her alive. She could see Simone tomorrow, after she'd safely ditched her persistent cop escort.

Besides, he *needed* her.

"Looks like it's your lucky day."

8

LUCKY?

Josh let the cool fall breeze wash over him and tried to figure that one out.

His best friend was going to kill him for having a one-night stand with Lexi. He'd just come up empty on his latest lead in the smuggling case. And he was further than ever from unearthing the bastards who trafficked in the corruption of wayward teenagers as much as the drug and weapons trade.

By all rights, it shouldn't feel like a lucky day.

But watching Lexi sashay her way past him across the Bertrands' lawn with a walk that sent her curves into enticing motion, Josh couldn't help but feel pretty damn fortunate. He'd never had much of a silver tongue, preferring action to talk any day. Yet somehow he'd convinced Ms. Independent to come with him when she was clearly dying to give her archenemy a piece of her mind.

"I don't suppose I could simply answer your questions about fashion in the car, and then you could let me go have my talk with Simone afterward?" She tapped her foot by the passenger door of his unmarked police vehicle.

Her perpetual motion automatically reminded him

of his efforts to keep her still last night. His body responded to the thought before he could edge an answer past his lips.

"I don't need to know about fashion, I need to know something about key players in the fashion industry. I'm trying to make sense of a case I'm working on, Lex." He unlocked the door for her and enjoyed the view as she slid inside. "It'll take more than a few minutes."

Josh walked around the standard issue, unmarked police vehicle and slid into the seat beside her.

"I'm helping you with your case?" She couldn't have sounded more delighted. Her eyes were wide, her hair wild after her time outdoors.

"No." He put the car into Drive and eased out of the Bertrands' circular driveway. "I just need to know something about the people you hang out with—designers and what not."

"And 'what not'?"

"You know, whoever it is that runs with the fashion crowd." Josh wound the car through the gated, private community and past multimillion-dollar homes.

"Models, photographers, high-society ladies—Simone's a designer *and* a high-society lady, by the way," Lexi clarified. "She was attending haute couture shows long before she ever tried creating something of her own."

"And your impression of her?"

"She's clueless and bitchy. I think you'll find that's everyone's impression of her."

It had been Josh's, too. Simone couldn't begin to mastermind a smuggling ring.

"What about you, Lexi? Are you a columnist and a high-society lady?" Sure, he needed information for his case, but because there was a chance Lexi could somehow be involved in the case—could even be in danger—Josh wanted to know something about her, too.

She snorted. "You saw where I live. It's a far cry from Simone's mansion."

"Property in Manhattan doesn't come cheap. And you seem to be on pretty familiar terms with the Bertrand family." He told himself he wasn't asking out of curiosity about Lexi. He needed to know so he could keep an eye on her this week while Duke was out of town.

Lexi wiggled in her seat, straightened her dress, recrossed her legs in the other direction.

His direction.

Josh's mouth went dry at the sight of her bare calves. She kicked her crossed leg in rhythmic motion, occasionally hitting the cord to his car radio and sending it swinging.

"I grew up in this neighborhood, but I was definitely never part of the 'ladies who lunch' crowd."

He waited, surprised by how much he wanted to hear more, know more, about Lexi.

"My parents are sought-after academics—Dad's a political scientist and Mom's an expert in Third World economics. We didn't move here until their books started selling and they began hiring themselves out on the national speaking circuit."

Josh noted the only people on the streets were lawn service workers and gardeners. His uncle still mowed lawns for a living. "Must be good money in political science."

"No. Even then, we lived in the gatekeeper's house at the beginning of the development." Lexi smoothed the fabric of her dress to her knee. "I was a bit of an outcast."

"At home, too?"

Her mouth fell open. "What kind of question is that?"

"Sorry." His stint as a smooth-talker had been short-lived. "I guess I was just thinking that your interests really diverged from your parents'."

"Meaning, their work has a lot more substance than fashion commentary?" She edged forward in her seat. Lexi on the defensive.

"Meaning that being a mover and shaker of pop culture is a far cry from academic studies of existing political and financial trends."

"Oh." She resettled against the black vinyl. "You think I'm a mover and a shaker?"

The way she worked that body of hers even when she was supposed to be sitting still reminded him she was a mover and shaker in more ways than one.

"That's exactly what you are."

"You've got me all figured out, don't you, Detective."

Her voice held a serious note that he hadn't heard from her before. The radio cord stopped swinging along with her foot.

He'd seen teasing Lexi, provocative Lexi and take-charge Lexi. But for a moment he caught a glimpse of another side.

"Not by half." He merged onto the highway, leaving the secluded Long Island neighborhood behind as he entered a world of mini-malls and fast-food restaurants. The expressway ran neck and neck with the raised train tracks that transported people into the city.

"Did you grow up in the city?" Lexi asked, whipping the strap of her purse from one side of her lap to the other.

The gentle slap of leather on her thighs was definitely not what he needed to hear right now.

"Brooklyn. My mother still lives there, but I've lived in Greenwich Village for the past ten years."

"Your dad?"

"Didn't we decide to keep things impersonal here?" Just because he'd needed to know a few things about her didn't mean he was ready to share his life story. And how could he concentrate on conversation, anyway, when the noise of that damn purse strap had him on the edge of his seat and ready to explode?

"You broke that rule when you started asking me questions that had nothing to do with key players in the fashion world."

Josh gritted his teeth, too wound up with sexual frustration to figure out a way around her questions. She'd make a great interrogator.

"My father remarried a long time ago, but he pretty much opted not to be a part of my life when he walked out on us."

"I hear you." Lexi nodded. "My parents both opted out of my life when I turned eighteen. I think the purple hair and matching leather pants finally pushed them over the edge."

"You're kidding." He wondered idly if she still owned any leather pants.

"My mother hates purple."

"I mean about your folks. You don't see much of them anymore?"

"They can be hard to reach in Zimbabwe, but I make an attempt every now and then." Lexi reshuffled her slender legs, crossing away from him now. Her arms laced across her chest. "New subject, please. How about we discuss this case of yours."

He recognized that it was time to retreat. He would dissect the new pieces of information he'd learned about Lexi later. The woman had worked her way into his system somehow, and he found himself needing to know more about her, wanting to see more of her.

But he also needed to pick her brain about his case while he had the chance. He wanted the men who'd corrupted kids into crime, the men who masterminded a smuggling operation that had logged thousands of police hours this summer. Talking about the case definitely made for safer territory than thoughts of Lexi in leather.

"How does Simone run her business if she's so clueless?"

"She doesn't. Anton handles all the business details so Simone can just play with her fabric swatches all day."

"Anton?"

"The gentleman in tennis whites you chased away with your snarl."

Shit. Josh had been too concerned with running off the guy to pay attention to how the guy might fit into the smuggling case. Despite Josh's best efforts to stay focused in his interview with Simone, Lexi's presence in the house had distracted him, made him careless.

"So he would take care of the books, contracting suppliers, shipping goods...." Maybe Lexi would be able to help dig him out from the hole he'd created, however. She did seem to know a lot about the fashion business.

No matter that she didn't share the same interests as her parents—Josh was willing to bet she'd inherited a sharp mind from her academic folks.

"Anton also schedules Simone for interviews with the media, sets up her shows, everything." Lexi tugged her long hair out from behind her and laid the dark mass over one shoulder.

Smart *and* sexy.

How the hell could he *not* get distracted by such a combination?

"What's Anton like?" He tried to separate his professional need for information from the unexpected personal sense of jealousy he'd experienced at the sight of Lexi talking so companionably with another man.

"Charming. Articulate. And he must be a little bit smarter than I'd first given him credit for, because his business sense seems to be helping Simone forge a profit in spite of herself."

He ignored the charming and articulate praise. Josh didn't need any more reasons to feel animosity toward the guy. Emotions could cloud the best professional judgment.

If Anton was at the helm of Simone's operation as a designer, then Josh needed to check him out first thing tomorrow. But right now, he needed to address the threat to his concentration.

He couldn't ignore her. If Anton Bertrand was involved in anything underhanded, Josh had more reason than ever to keep an eye on Lexi. Instead of worrying about Lexi's ability to rob him of all focus, what would happen if he focused on her?

Perhaps another night with Lexi would excise the relentless hunger for her that screwed up his concentration and wreaked havoc on his ability to effectively question a suspect.

Hell, he'd already guaranteed himself a spot on Duke's personal hit list when his partner returned to town. What would it hurt if Josh spent one more night with the siren who could shift from dominatrix jailer to teasing captive and set his bloodstream on fire while she was at it?

Assuming, of course, he could talk her into one more night. One more night with a lot more condoms.

He glanced over at her, wondering how he could entice New York's most talked-about fashion columnist into re-crossing her legs in his direction.

Last night, Lexi Mansfield had stalked him through a trendy Manhattan bar like a professional predator. Maybe tonight, it was his turn to launch his own hot pursuit.

LEXI KNEW from personal experience that long lapses in conversation meant the other party was losing interest. As a child, her enthusiasm and energy had often been met with extended silence. As an adult, she worked hard to deliver her best writing every week so that her audience would always be entertained and engaged. A critic she could handle.

What she couldn't stand was being ignored.

She huffed a stray strand of kinky hair out of her eyes. "Feel free to drop me off at the next train stop. You seem to have wrested all the information you needed from me."

She idly poked at the window crank with the toes of her crossed leg, disappointed to lose her audience, but telling herself that she needed to distance herself from the raw sensual appeal Josh held for her.

She liked her ivory tower—the safe haven of her home office, the companionship of friends and pets—just fine. Why would she risk her emotional well-being on a moody, albeit very tempting, cop? Especially when all of New York already seemed to think she was the world's least appealing woman.

The last thing she needed was to have the assessment confirmed.

"Trust me." Josh's voice stole into her thoughts, drawing her back to their conversation. "I haven't wrested half of what I want from you yet."

Surely he'd meant for her to take those words at face value. It was only her heightened awareness of Josh that made her read something sensual into the sentiment.

"Why don't you tell me what else you need?" She cleared her throat of the sudden husky hunger lurking there, scarcely noticing that they'd pulled up in front of her building.

He jammed the car into Park and slipped two cool, heavy metallic rings onto her lap. From the weight and the circular shape, Lexi knew what she would find perched on her thighs.

Josh swiveled in his seat to face her. "Why don't you see for yourself?"

Warm desire flooded her veins. She probably wouldn't ever be able to look at a pair of handcuffs without blushing. Good God, what had she been thinking last night to do all those naughty—glorious—things with Josh?

The heavy metal weighted her light dress, causing the cuffs to insinuate themselves in the hollow of her lap. Fragmentary visions of her body entwined with Josh's charged full force into her brain.

It didn't help that he was seated little more than a foot away. Lexi could see the tiny diamond stud earring that had raked lightly against her thigh last night. She could smell the aftershave that had just barely lingered on her pillows this morning.

And the scar. What woman's pulse wouldn't pound at the sight of a scar that announced to the whole world that this man could fight his way out of any dark alley and live to tell the tale?

Lexi fought the urge to lick her lips. Josh was probably only making the overture because she'd been a little carried away last night and had ended up behaving like a porn queen.

He hadn't seen the real her. He didn't know a damn

thing about her. And if he did, handcuff playtime would be over in a heartbeat.

Lexi collected the cuffs and slid them across the police cruiser's vinyl bench seat. "I don't think so."

The words felt as if they were being torn from her almost against her will, but she wouldn't let her heart be broken by some guy who only wanted a wild ride.

"You still don't want to make things personal?" Josh's thick, tanned fingers flexed around the metal rings, but he didn't reveal any other reaction to her rejection.

"I'm not in the market for a relationship right now." The sentiment sounded trite to her ears, as it no doubt would to his. But she meant every word— no matter how tempting it might be to fantasize about another night with Josh.

"Lord, woman, you sound like a New Yorker. What does that mean, you're not in the market? I wasn't looking to make a business deal, I just wanted a chance to get to know you."

She sniffed. Fluffed her hair. Erected general emotional armor. "Despite my behavior last night, I don't consider playing with handcuffs to be a genuine date."

"Are you saying you used me as your personal sex toy?"

His voice floated over her like a warm wave, drowning her in sensual memories.

"I'm saying, let's not complicate things with more erotic interludes." Her cheeks had to be flaming. She'd never need to buy blush again if she spent much time around this man.

She pretended great interest in scenery outside the car window.

"Be honest with me, Lex."

Josh's hand crept over her knee and rested there. The gesture contained a sensual element, as any touch from him always would, yet it soothed her nerves and calmed her jumpy insides, too.

"Don't spout the 'let's not complicate things' mantra. Just shoot it to me straight. Are you scared of this thing between us? Of me?"

"I am *not* scared of you." She crossed her fingers that he would move on to another topic, that her vehement denial would distract him from this line of questioning.

"So you're scared of us?"

Damn it. She should have known a cop wouldn't be thrown off the trail that easily.

"Us? There is no 'us,' Josh." She scrambled to interest him in another topic before her heavy breathing fogged up the windows.

"You *are* scared."

"And that's such a big revelation to you? I invite a total stranger back to my place one night, play erotic games in the dark with him, and then wake up to discover his best friend is engaged to my best friend. Of course I am scared to get any more involved with you."

"Why? Because Amanda won't like you anymore if you give me the boot? Come on, Lex, we can handle our friends—"

Was it her imagination, or did his expression suggest he wasn't quite as convinced of this as he'd have her believe?

"Besides, a woman who can play dominatrix to a room full of gossipmongering snobs can handle her own best friend."

"Maybe I'm not the woman you think I am." He was circling too close, invading boundaries she'd kept well protected.

"You're not the stalker in black sequins who hauled a veteran vice cop around by the nose last night?" Josh probed her gaze, seeming to see right through her.

Nervous energy filled her, making it almost impossible not to fidget.

"Well?"

"No. I'm not that woman. I'm actually a sequined fraud clinging to a name I've carved out for myself in high society. I'm a middle-class girl trying to make it with the blue bloods and I don't dare slip up for fear I'll lose my magazine forum, all my clout, and my ability to rake in big bucks for charities that don't have any other access to New York's deepest pockets."

The words probably surprised her more than they seemed to shock him. Until she'd blurted it out in a moment of panic, she hadn't fully realized the scope of the pressure she put on herself.

Josh opened his mouth to respond, but Lexi wasn't finished yet.

"So yes, I'm scared of messing up. I'm scared of complicating things. And I'm scared of freaky people who threaten me to keep my mouth shut in my column.'' Lexi pressed on, eager to talk through her new revelation, for her own sake more than his. ''But most of all, I'm scared of carrying the public persona of Lexi Mansfield into my private life for fear I'll be consumed by her. And she is most definitely *not* me.''

''Wait a minute.'' Josh frowned so deeply the scar on his temple wrinkled. ''First of all, I think your public persona is more a real part of you than you think. You are definitely not a fraud, Lexi. But right now, I need you to go back to the part about freaky people who threaten you to keep your mouth shut. What is that all about?''

''Did I say that?'' She'd internalized her fears about the anonymous letters for so many weeks, she'd almost forgotten the rest of the world didn't know about them.

''Yes, you said that. Who is threatening you?''

''It's really not a big deal—''

''Who?'' His voice lacked the patience, the humor, that had marked their conversations in the past.

Lexi didn't mind quite so much, seeing his warrior spirit spring to the fore on her account.

''I don't know. I've been receiving anonymous letters for the past few weeks, but they are computer generated and pretty vague, so I—''

''Your best friend is engaged to a cop, as you've already been quick to point out to me.'' A tick started in his eye, twitching the scar in an even rhythm. ''Why the hell didn't you tell him? Or her, for that matter?''

Lexi stiffened. ''How do you know I didn't, hot-shot?''

"Because Duke wouldn't have left town if he'd known. Or he would have told me about the damn letters when he called this morning and asked me to check on you."

"Why would Duke Rawlins ask you to check on me?" Her life seemed to be unraveling before her eyes. First, Josh's overture to see her again and all the emotional implications a relationship posed. Then he made it sound like the anonymous letters were something really serious. Now she had cops secretly checking up on her.

"Because your friends are starting to overlap with the case we're working on, Lexi, and the players involved are a lot more dangerous than your poisoned-pen friend, Simone. Do you think maybe she wrote the letters?"

"Why would she threaten me anonymously when she's obviously not afraid to tell me off publicly?" Was it her imagination, or had he moved closer? He loomed near, crowding her in the car's front seat.

"Maybe she thought she'd hedge her bets. What exactly do these letters threaten?"

"Me. My dogs." She didn't like to think about the notes. Part of her kept hoping they were the sort of thing anyone with a little celebrity would receive. There were always a few malcontents that didn't like her columns. Her nervous fingers played with the strap of her purse, flipping it from side to side.

Josh tugged the strap out of her hands and held her hands still. "You're showing me all these letters and filing a complaint."

"Do you really think that's necessary?" Her heart

sped up a little more the closer he got. At this rate, she'd need medication by the time they got out of the car.

"I can't believe they threatened Muffin and you're just letting them walk all over you."

"Well, I—" She was so confused, so…aroused… she wasn't even thinking straight.

"And I'm coming up with you to check out your apartment's security."

"My building is very safe, Josh." She did *not* need him in her apartment. She'd jump him in ten seconds flat.

He was already out of the car, however, and coming around to her side to open the door. Lexi's pulse fluttered, her knees threatened no support if she were to stand now.

He pried open her door and offered one broad palm for assistance.

"No, Lexi. *I'm* safe. Anything less than me is not enough protection." He tugged her out onto the street, his body brushing hers briefly before he shut the door behind her.

Had he meant to do that?

The look he flashed her was innocent enough.

Still…

Lexi stared at the earringed man with a scar who was supposed to be so damn safe. He looked more like a bloodthirsty pirate transported from a ship deck to the driver's seat of an unmarked Ford.

"But once you're done securing my apartment, you have to leave." She wanted to settle that up front.

He cast her a quick glance, his light gray eyes reminding her he wasn't bloodthirsty—just hungry for her.

"Maybe once I'm done securing your apartment, you won't want me to."

9

_____

"A LITTLE SURE of yourself aren't you, Winger?"

The words had plenty of bite to them, but Josh hardly noticed as Lexi wriggled from foot to foot beneath his intent stare. The whole ride back to the city had been an exercise in slow torture, and Lexi's restless movements didn't do a damn thing to help him remain in control.

"Maybe. Or maybe I'm just an optimist."

Even she had to recognize that his car had crackled with tangible attraction the whole way from Long Island to Manhattan. Why would she deny herself the kind of off-the-charts pleasure they'd generated last night? After all, Josh would be the one taking all the heat for their relationship. Lexi didn't have to work with Duke every day.

Was she really scared of starting something with him? Could she be insecure underneath that balls-to-the-wall attitude she carried around with her as surely as her leopard-print purse?

Her feet seemed to dance in place on the pavement, but he wasn't giving her any room to get around him yet. He wondered if her toenails were still painted bright blue under those semi-conservative heels.

"Trust me, Winger, you don't look anything like a

Pollyanna. I'm thinking you're just way too cocksure for your own good."

He groaned at her choice of words. Judging from her cat-who-ate-the-canary grin, the words were no doubt deliberate. He grew ten times harder just hearing the damn phrase fall from her pouty lips.

"You're in trouble now." He pulled her behind him to cross West Sixty-second Street and head toward her building. He needed privacy with her. Fast.

"Actually, I'm not even sure I'm going to invite you in."

He turned on her so fast she ran into him. Her sweet body plastered itself to his for all of two seconds before she peeled herself off and stepped back.

His voice rasped with the effort of talking over his rampant case of lust. "You're definitely inviting me in. I'm on official police business until I've got those letters of yours in my hands."

Her eyes widened just a fraction.

"Fine." The word was breathless. "But that's all I'm putting in your hands today."

He envisioned the way she'd given herself to him so completely last night. More than anything, he wanted to share that with her again. "You're calling the shots, lady."

Her gaze narrowed. "You're sure?"

"How about we say that if you want anything else from me, you're going to have to ask. I'm not presuming a thing once we go upstairs." He didn't mention that he would keep the power of persuasion in his back pocket, however.

"So if I thought a goodbye kiss would be okay…"

"You're going to have to initiate it."

From the mixture of surprise and anticipation in her eyes, Josh wondered how much experience she'd had taking the initiative.

"And if I decided to live on the edge and go for a repeat of last night?" She twisted and untwisted the strap of her bag around her finger.

If the constant wriggle of her restless body didn't do him in, the leather strap of her purse definitely would.

"You're going to have to convince me that's what you really want." He needed her to realize she wanted this, too.

"Oh." Her eyes went soft and warm. Her bag slipped from her hand and hit the street pavement with a soft *thud*.

"Shall we go inside?" Josh recovered her bag and placed it gently in her hand. He tried not to notice the exotic floral scent of her, the slight heat of her body jump-starting the fragrance that had barely teased his nose until now.

Teasing her was going to be far more torturous for him than it would be for her. But he wanted her to be a part of this, too. He wouldn't be satisfied with an impersonal erotic interlude in the dark anymore, as ludicrous as that sounded when he wanted her so badly he couldn't see straight.

Yet he knew Lexi had so much more to offer, so much more she probably hadn't even afforded herself. He wanted to take her deeper into realms of pleasure she'd never explored. Maybe she'd realize she was stronger than she gave herself credit for, capable of sustaining a relationship without compromising her career or her goals.

Not that he was going so far as to say he wanted to be the man for her. Although, now that he thought about it, he sure as hell wouldn't envision her with any other man.

Maybe he *was* the man for her, at least for right now.

Now all he had to do was prove it.

LEXI'S LEGS WOBBLED as she moved toward her building. For a woman who'd practically been born in high heels, the condition said a lot about Josh's effect on her.

God, she wanted him.

She wanted to explore his big, burly shoulders with her hands. She wanted to taste the hollow at the base of his throat, to inhale the all-male scent of him. She wanted to hear the *thump* of his heart beneath her ear, to trace her finger through the whorls of hair she'd felt on his chest.

Most of all, she just wanted to see him.

Last night had been over-the-top exciting in the pitch blackness. But today, all she could think about was catching a glimpse of Josh in the light—as nature had made him.

He held the door for her and flashed a wicked grin.

His gaze strayed south, flicking over her breasts. They responded immediately, visibly, through her lightweight dress.

"I hope you're thinking about me," he half growled, half whispered in her ear as she charged through the door, head held high despite her carnal thoughts.

"I never said I wasn't going to think about you," she admitted, now that she was thoroughly caught. "I'm just not going to act on it."

They stepped onto an empty elevator, and Lexi pressed the button for her floor.

Josh leaned close to whisper in her ear. "Want to know what I'm thinking about right now?"

"No." She shivered anyway, certain Josh's thoughts were as impure as her own.

"According to our rules, though, I think I'm technically allowed to talk about what I'd like—I just can't actually give it to you." Josh scrubbed his stubbled jaw with one hand and studied her, as if genuinely trying to remember the specifics of their agreement.

He looked wily as a fox with those sexy gray eyes. Lexi would wager her wardrobe that he knew exactly what he was doing to her with his provocative conversation.

The elevator cabin seemed smaller, suddenly, and Josh's presence dominated the intimate space.

The fabric of her dress clung to her, caressing her sensitized flesh and frustrating her with its wispy touch. She became very aware of her lack of stockings. Her bare thighs pressed together in an effort to assuage the sweet ache his presence inspired.

"You are a wicked man, Josh Winger," she managed to say, her voice husky with the effort of holding herself back.

His gaze held her captive as surely as if he'd touched her.

"Not half as wicked as I'd like right now."

Thank God the elevator doors swished open when they did, or she might have caved to the close quarters and heated atmosphere.

She needed to insert some distance between them, fast, if she was going to survive this "official police business" visit. Drawing lines only seemed to tempt the man to cross them, so Lexi scavenged her brain for another tact. How did one send a man running?

Inspiration struck as she turned the key in her front door lock.

"I can't help but wonder where those wicked ways came from." She nudged open the door with her shoulder and was greeted by a chorus of happy barking. "I've bared my whole childhood to you, Detective, but you haven't told me a thing about your past."

That stern jaw of his slackened just a little. His eyes widened. He didn't look stricken exactly...but he definitely looked like a man caught in a surprise attack.

"Nothing to tell." He scooped up her fluffy white shih tzu who seemed to have taken a liking to Josh. "What's this one's name?"

"That's Snowball." Lexi bent to pet her other dogs in an effort to hide a smile. Poor Josh was in major retreat mode. "But I don't even know if you grew up in the city, or—"

"Snowball?" Josh grimaced even as he stroked the dog's downy head. "How can this dog hold his head up on the streets of New York with a name like Snowball? I bet he's embarrassed to even go out for a walk.''

''*She* is not one bit embarrassed. She happens to love her bows and her color-coordinated collars.'' Lexi pointed to her gray terrier. ''I gave Harry a 'guy' name because he's a boy. And I almost never put a bow on him unless it's a special occasion, in which case he seems amenable to a bow-tie collar.''

''Please tell me you're joking.''

Josh set down Snowball, much to her dismay, and gave Harry a sympathetic pat on the back.

''At least Harry is a good name.''

''Thanks. What sorts of names do the kids in your family have?'' The segue was weak, but it worked. Besides, she wasn't just trying to torment Josh, she really wanted to know something about this man who seemed determined to invade her life at all levels. ''Or do you even have brothers and sisters?''

''You're relentless.''

''I know.'' She tossed her leopard-print purse on a curio table, shoved off her shoes, and moved into the kitchen. ''But make yourself comfortable while you tell me all about yourself—and if you don't leave out any of the good parts, I'll make you the best cup of cappuccino you've ever had.''

''You know, I'm here for those letters, not for chit-chat, Lexi.''

Instead of making himself comfortable, he opted to follow her right into the kitchen, his big body making the room seem much too small.

He might have been able to scare off a lesser woman with that glower on his face, but Lexi wasn't fooled for a minute. She was warming up to her role as the interrogating officer.

If only he didn't crowd her so much. Heat her flesh with his stare. Light her fire just by standing next to her.

"Chitchat first, letters later." She ground the coffee and pulled out the cappuccino maker, determined not to lose ground.

"I've got a family full of stepsisters and stepbrothers in both directions, but no blood siblings." Josh stalked out of the kitchen and around her living room furniture like a bear in Goldilocks's house. He finally chose the chair shaped like a giant clam and folded his big body into it.

"Meaning both your parents remarried?" Now that she had room to breathe again, she searched her cabinets for the cinnamon while the milk heated.

"Mom moved to the suburbs to live the American Dream in upstate, and Pop still lives in an iffy section of Brooklyn. They're antagonistic as hell toward one another, but basically happy with their lives now that they're not married."

As much as Lexi struggled to have a relationship with her happily married parents, she knew it had to be ten times as difficult to relate to an embittered mother and father. "Do you see them much?"

"I don't have anything to say to my dad since he walked out on my mother, so I don't ever see him. I see my mom, but I'm sort of a reminder of unhappier times for her, so I give her lots of space." He stretched forward in his chair to try to see what she was doing in the kitchen. "I hope you've got something more substantial than just cappuccino over there, because I'm pouring out my heart just like you asked.''

She flashed his trademark glower right back at him. "Keep talking, Winger, or you'll never see those letters."

"Jeez, woman, you're scary."

"No kidding. I learned that look from the most fearsome guy I know." She tossed a few cookies on a plate and brought them into the living room to soothe him. "How'd you get the scar?"

He didn't answer until he'd eaten two cookies; of course, that took all of ten seconds.

"A broken beer bottle from a long-ago fight—and that's as much as you're getting out of me today."

"How old were you when this fight occurred?" Lexi poured their cappuccino and brought him a mug.

Josh was already on his feet, strolling around her aquatic-themed living room and absently touching whatever was in reach. He surfed two fingers along the rim of the fish tank, rolled his thumb over a portrait of her from her college days at Columbia.

Lexi could almost feel that caress on her face.

"Seventeen, I think. But you should have seen the other guy." He sighed as if the weight of the world were on his big shoulders. "I mean it, Lex. No more questions."

"Please tell me you didn't opt to use broken glass on your opponent." She sipped her drink, wondering how she'd moved from thinking last night that she shouldn't let a stranger in her apartment to companionably discussing the sordid past of this rough-and-tumble guy whose life sounded too close to *The Sopranos* for comfort.

Maybe the strangest aspect of it all was that she felt utterly comfortable with him here, even without hiding from him in the dark the way she had last night.

Of course, *comfortable* probably wasn't the right word for what she was feeling. Anytime she had a visual on this guy, Lexi experienced a wave of excitement; a sense of anticipation that was never far from the surface.

Good thing she knew how to keep herself too distracted to think about that.

"So? Was your weapon of choice a bottle, or not?"

JOSH HAD HER NOW. He heard the curiosity in her voice, knew the journalist in her would want her questions answered.

He spun on her and smiled. "Letters first, chitchat later."

She huffed a noisy sigh and plunked her mug on the coffee table. "Fine. But I wouldn't push my luck much further if I were you, Winger." She stormed off into another room, her walk quieter now that she'd ditched her heels.

"Why's that?" he called, listening to her rustling around the bedroom.

"Because I've got a pack of wild dogs at my disposal in case I decide you've annoyed me too much." Her voice grew louder as she walked back into the living room. "Snowball might look like a lady, but she's a scrapper if you back her into a corner."

Snowball currently gazed up at him adoringly through a veil of fluffy white fur and a lopsided bow.

"I'll bet." Josh filched the handful of papers in Lexi's hands and settled on a stool painted to look like bright orange coral. He started shuffling through the pages, scattering the notes along the counter dividing the kitchen from the living room.

"Well?" Lexi prodded.

Josh studied the words on the paper and absorbed several superficial things. They'd been printed on an inkjet printer. The salutations never used Lexi's first name, instead calling her "Ms. Mansfield." The papers smelled like Lexi's perfume, and she had meticulously stamped each of them with a "Date Received" mark as if it were business correspondence.

"Well, what?"

"Glass or no glass?"

"I hit the glass out of the other guy's hands with a stick, but then I gave him an old-fashioned beating with the most tried-and-true weapons of all."

"Your fists?"

She sounded so worried that Josh spared a glance in her direction. She was hanging on every word of the ancient history of that stupid scar. Why couldn't she be interested in spending tonight with him instead of concerning herself with a night long ago?

Josh rubbed an absent finger along the marred line of skin on his cheek as he continued reading the threats to Lexi. "Yeah. But the broken beer bottle had been meant for Mary Alice Delaney after she broke up with this guy. So I thought the fists were sort of justified."

Damn, he didn't like what he was reading.

"I'm taking these into the station for analysis, Lex. But first, you're going to have to give me some specifics on where and how you received all of them."

And then, after he'd secured all the information he needed to track down Lexi's letter writer, Josh would get back to the real task at hand.

Convincing Lexi to let him stay.

10

HALF AN HOUR LATER, after answering Josh's every picky question about the hows and whys of each threatening letter, Lexi couldn't concentrate on the interrogation anymore. Her gaze fixed on the scar creasing Josh's rugged mug. She kept thinking about the story behind it, her heart touched by the notion of Josh defending his ideals and anyone weaker than him, even as a seventeen-year-old.

They were seated on the coral stools pulled up to her kitchen counter, empty cappuccino mugs between them.

"I hope Mary Alice Delaney realized how lucky she was to have you there to protect her." She couldn't help the emotion welling up in her voice.

Josh closed his eyes. Sighed. "Actually, I think she was too busy calling the cops on us to pay much attention to my great heroic deed."

"You're kidding. You didn't get in trouble, did you?"

He carefully scooped up all the letters in a pile and tucked them into a plastic bag he withdrew from a pocket inside his jacket. Safely stowed, he stuffed the small package back into his pocket.

Lexi smiled to see a quick flash of his broad chest

beneath the jacket, a tantalizing expanse of cotton T-shirt over mouth-watering muscle.

"I spent the night in jail—" he talked right over her outraged gasp "—but it was a good experience. It made me realize I wanted to be a cop." He shoved the stool away from the counter and stood. "Speaking of which, a good cop would make sure your home is secure in light of these threats, Lex."

"My home has always been my haven. I feel very safe here."

Ignoring her, he peered around her door, lifted silk moiré window treatments, and poked the call button on her intercom. He frowned, furrowed his brow— did all the things that made him look twice as scary as normal.

"I'll talk to the building superintendent about a few things before I leave you here alone, but overall it looks pretty good. Do you have any idea how to defend yourself, Lexi?"

She spun off her stool and stood to face him. "I didn't spend six weeks of my life sacrificing Tuesday nights at the Y for nothing, I assure you."

He edged closer, crowded her. "Is that right?"

Desire for Josh—hunger she'd scarcely managed to suppress since they'd set foot in her apartment— roared back to life with a vengeance. His blatant disregard for her personal boundaries brought the physical chemistry issue between them into sudden, sharp focus.

"That's right." Lexi fended him off with a trademark bad girl stance, hoping he wouldn't see the slight wobble of her legs at such close range.

Josh's mouth curved around a predatory smile. He stepped so close, Lexi thought—hoped—for one crazy moment that he would embrace her.

He leaned a fraction nearer to whisper, his words fanning soft and warm on her cheek. ''Then, let's see what you've got.''

The request had barely registered before Josh turned from seductive fantasy man to role-playing attacker. He flipped her around and pulled her back up against him, one of his forearms pinning her at the waist, the other covering her mouth to prevent a scream.

Her heart pounded with the sudden rush of adrenaline, not from fear, but from fierce, primal arousal. She knew without a doubt she could go slack against him and have her way with this delicious man inside of ten seconds.

But she wasn't just the pampered uptown girl he thought she was, and maybe it was about time Josh Winger realized as much. Besides, what if her letter writer really did accost her? Better to practice her skills now, on a safe target like Josh.

Taking a deep breath, Lexi stepped backward in a single quick move, planting one foot between both of his. She dug her fingers into the arm around her waist and bent forward, hauling the massive police detective over her body to land him flat on his back in the middle of her living room.

Muffin and Harry howled their approval, while Snowball sniffed nervously around Josh's face. The little shih tzu cast an accusing bark at Lexi.

Josh's eyes were closed. Dear God, she hadn't meant to hurt him.

"Are you okay?" Lexi knelt beside the fallen giant.

"I'm not sure." As he pried open one gray eye, his hand snaked out to lightly graze the back of her thigh through her skirt. "Why don't you come closer and we'll find out."

Her skin tingled, tightened underneath his fingers. She wasn't supposed to let this happen, but his touch felt so good, so right.

"You told me you would behave unless I asked you not to, remember?"

"I think all bets are off once you started man-handling me." He rolled onto his side, still stretched out on the turquoise carpet in her living room, but his hand fell away from her leg. "Did you honestly learn that move at the Y?"

Lexi mourned the loss of his touch, wondering why she bothered to fight a man whose slightest proximity gave her goose bumps.

"Yes. They offer lots of classes, and I'd heard self-defense was a good course to take for people with self-esteem issues." She was already in too deep. She might as well put her cards on the table.

"You? Self-esteem issues?" He plucked one of her curls from her shoulder and rubbed it between his fingers.

"Who would think, right?" Lexi moved to stand, but Josh held her fast with one arm.

Josh wanted to ask her more about the self-esteem thing. Lexi could tell by the probing look in his gray eyes. They stared at one another, locked in a momentary battle of wills that mirrored their physical match.

She bit her lip, not wanting to tread on that particular territory tonight. Josh's eyes darted to the gesture, and—oddly—seemed to relent.

His voice growled over her. "Double or nothing, I bet you can't pin me."

She mentally thanked him for letting her off the hook. "What is this, WrestleMania?"

"I'll give you a handicap of a three-second head start." He let go of her wrist but edged closer, using his big body to nudge her into playing his game.

"Are you really that concerned about my safety, Detective, or is this just an excuse to roll around the floor and tangle limbs?"

He hoisted himself up to a sitting position. "You're losing precious seconds here." That predatory smile of his made a comeback. "Come on, Lexi, show me your moves."

Her heart thundered in her ears, pounded in her chest. He was giving her permission to jump him. She'd be a fool not to take him up on it.

His thigh grazed hers as he moved over her, angling his body above hers in the most dominant of positions. "You're gonna be at my mercy if you don't act now, lady."

His whispered words called to mind erotic delights that made her shiver. Yet he still wasn't touching her. A brush here, a slight skim there, no more.

Was she moving away from his advancing pursuit, she wondered, or merely making herself comfortable on the floor for what she really wanted?

"And once you're at my mercy—" he walked his fingers up the outside of her thigh "—the first thing I'm doing is checking to see if those are really leopard-print panties you're wearing."

Heat flooded her thighs, ignited a restless ache for him.

"How did you know they were leopard-print?" Did that husky voice really belong to her?

He cupped a hand around her hipbone, his fingers gently squeezing the soft flesh of her bottom. "I staked out a good angle when I helped you into the car. Your dresses are much too short, Lexi."

"Either that, or your eyes are much too well trained."

"Could be." His body extended completely over hers, his weight held off her by one elbow.

The heat, the hunger became much too much to bear.

She thought about rolling Josh to his back and teasing him within an inch of losing his mind, but a sensual languor infused her limbs, made her whole body heavy with delicious anticipation.

"Pin me," she whispered.

JOSH'S GROAN startled the little dog Harry into a quick *yap* from the mat by the front door, but Lexi's other dogs stayed mercifully unaware as they lay near one another in the hallway.

Good. He had enough fish smiling at him from the painted seascape along Lexi's baseboards without adding any canine voyeurs to the mix.

Lowering only a portion of his weight onto Lexi, Josh pinned her to the aqua carpet.

Her sigh of satisfaction hissed along his neck. "Yessss."

"Better?"

She arched her back to press herself more deeply into him. "Mmm."

"Are you okay here, on the floor?" He didn't want her to think he had no control—that he couldn't have made it as far as the bedroom. It would be painful to have to step away from her for even the ten seconds it would take to get back to the jungle headquarters and break through the mosquito netting, but for her, Josh would fight the battle.

"Don't you dare move anywhere except to take off these clothes." The threat in her tone was unmistakable.

He mentally blessed her impatience, then eased his hand under the hem of her dress. "These clothes?"

Lexi tugged his shirttail out of his pants. "No, these clothes. This time, I want to see everything I missed out on in the dark."

Lifting off his shirt, Josh couldn't help but smile. "Honey, you pretty much get the best of this guy in the dark."

Lexi licked her full lips, her gaze locked on his bare chest. Her eyes roved, lingered, practically killed him with their thorough inspection.

"I beg to differ with you there." She smoothed her fingers over the planes of his chest, circling the myriad scars forged in half a lifetime on the police force with the gentle rake of one manicured nail. "In my line of work, I see physical perfection so often it makes me ill.'' She paused in her intense perusal to meet his gaze. ''Did you know we are cultivating an era full of plastic dolls? I swear every chick on the runway this season has the exact same pixie nose, and the men are no better. Everyone popped out of the same flawless mold.''

Her restless fingers followed his as he unzipped his pants.

He couldn't suppress a shudder of reaction when her nail flicked lightly over his hip. ''You won't find that problem here,'' he said through clenched teeth as he shoved the rest of his clothes down his legs and off his feet.

''You're right. Your proportions are all off.'' She wasted no time reversing their positions. Rolling on top of him, she pinned him to the floor with her slight weight. Her eyes shifted down his body and lingered.

A smile broke out across her face as her hands slipped between them to curve around his erection. ''Take this, for instance. Very impressive, Detective.''

He didn't stand a chance in hell of answering. She sat on top of him like Venus on the damn mountaintop, a Cheshire cat grin curling her lips.

''Like that, Josh?''

''You've got about ten seconds to get undressed before I'm hunting down the handcuffs, woman.''

Undaunted, she moved her hand up and down the length of him, exquisite torture administered by a five-foot dominatrix. ''Haven't I taught you anything about playing nice? I thought all that time in the jail cell would have taught you not to snarl.''

An explosion was imminent. He was going to lose it right now if he didn't tip Venus off her throne and gain control again on top. Neither seemed like a good option, but then—bless the little siren—she reached for the hem of her dress and started to pull it up.

Maybe he could hold on just one more minute....

Leopard-print panties came into view just in time. He called upon new reserves of strength to stick around for this show. He hadn't had the chance to see all of her body last night, but he'd spent all day imagining what she looked like. The fantasy hadn't been nearly this good.

Lexi's golden skin blended right into the background color of the panties. Her belly was sleek and smooth, her hips small but gently flared.

He held his breath as the dress kept moving up. Finally, a scrap of leopard-print silk announced the unveiling of her breasts. Insubstantial triangle patches of fabric stayed connected by skimpy straps. The whole contraption looked temptingly easy to unfasten, sort of like swiping away a spiderweb with one finger.

As she tossed her dress aside, Josh lifted his hand to touch her.

''Not so fast.'' She dipped two of her fingers under one bra strap and tugged it partway down her shoulders. ''I'm still in the driver's seat here.''

He plotted revenge in the form of multiple orgasms, and kept his eyes glued to those scraps of silk.

''I'm prepared to reward good behavior,'' she whispered, her breathy voice at its most sultry. ''Do you know any sweet talk to make a girl feel good, tough guy?''

He couldn't have salivated more over a ten-course meal as he waited for that silk to move a fraction of an inch. His throat rasped with hunger, thirst and desire. ''You're gorgeous.''

''Mmm. That'll do.'' She tugged the strap the rest of the way down her shoulder, unveiling the first course.

Josh couldn't stop himself if he tried—he had to disrupt their positions, had to sit up to take a taste of what she offered.

Lexi moaned, shifted, sighed. Her soft words of encouragement urged him on, assured him he wasn't being totally selfish. She tasted so clean, so sweet. The scrap of silk beneath her breast caught on his stubbled cheek, teased his skin along with her silky flesh.

''Josh, *please*.''

Sweeter words were never spoken.

Josh reached back to search out a condom from his pants pocket, juggling Lexi on his lap. Once he was sheathed, all he had to do was tug the little ties on the sides of her panties and watch them fall away from her slender hips. He vowed to buy her a whole drawer full of these clever contraptions.

She was warm and naked against him, seated across his lap. All he had to do was lift her up…just a little farther.

''Oh.'' Lexi hammered on his shoulder with one lax fist as he slid his way inside her. ''Yessss.''

Her slick heat surrounded him, drove him closer to

the brink he'd fought all night. She squeezed him closer with surprising strength, drawing his lips unerringly to her breast.

Gladly, he unhooked the rest of her leopard-patterned undergarments. He took his time drawing tight circles around each nipple with his tongue, teasing and rewarding them in turn.

He lifted her on top of him, sliding in and out of her body in slow, seductive rhythm.

By the time he reached between them to seek out the source of her pleasure, Lexi was breathing hard, her body quivering.

He drew a slow circle around that delicate nub with his thumb, perfectly mirroring the sweep of his tongue around her nipple. Her body tensed, arched. With only that one slow circle, Lexi flew apart around him.

Her body squeezed his, drawing an answering detonation inside him. His release thundered through him like a freight train, as if he'd somehow poured all of his heart and soul into Lexi.

In the long minutes afterward, as he held her through the warm aftershocks, Josh couldn't help but wonder—and worry—that maybe he had.

MAKING LOVE with the light on had definite benefits as far as Lexi was concerned.

For one thing, the floor of her living room gave her the impression that she'd just had an erotic romp ten leagues under the sea. And she had to admit she felt sultry as a mermaid now, with her arms and hair tangled around Josh.

She stared up at the best benefit of illuminated sex.

Josh Winger lay with his eyes closed beside her, his face only marginally less severe in repose. Something about the bold slash of his eyebrows, the chiseled angles of his cheekbones, hinted at the fierce street warrior lurking within.

But Lexi had discovered there was more to this man than amazing pecs and a take-no-prisoners glower. Josh was also her staunch protector, an unlikely ally. Her household full of pets hadn't scared him off, her wild fashion sense and penchant for speaking her mind hadn't sent him running, and—best of all—even her high-visibility career didn't seem to faze him.

Was there a chance she had room in her life for a man, after all? A man who wouldn't feel threatened by her success, yet would respect what she did?

An idea jumped into her head, teased the corners of her mind. "Josh?"

"Hmm?" He cocked one eye open as he twisted a lock of her hair around and around his finger.

"I have to go to a black-tie dinner next weekend, the Dance for Children. Actually, I'm hosting the event and wondered—" She was surprised at the wave of nervousness that assailed her just before she asked him. She never had a problem speaking her mind, but she also had zero practice asking a man out.

But they'd just spent the past two nights together. And heaven knew, Josh had been the one to pursue her today. He couldn't be totally uninterested, could he?

Swallowing her nerves, she forged ahead. "Would you go with me as my date?"

"Lady, I'd go just about anywhere with you." He turned toward her in half sleep, his eyes falling closed again as he cupped the small of her back. "But I still do undercover work. I can't afford to have my mug splashed all over the society pages."

Gently, he stroked her hair, his movements growing slower as he neared sleep. But his words had robbed the gesture of its intended effect. Lexi didn't feel anything close to soothed as she lay wide awake, her bare body partially wrapped in the chenille throw Josh had filched from the back of her couch.

He wouldn't go with her.

"Are you okay with that?"

The quiet alertness in his voice caught her off guard. She thought he'd fallen asleep, but as she peered up at him, she found him studying her with an intensity any other woman would probably find disconcerting. Lexi, on the other hand, adored his eyes on her.

Usually, anyway. Right now, she wished she had covered her emotions better before she'd met that gray gaze, wished she had time to erase the husky sadness from her throat.

"Um. No. I'm not, actually."

Tender in spite of his blatant refusal to embrace her publicly, Josh pulled the throw over her, smoothing its contours to follow the lines of her body.

She batted his hands away, needing to distance herself from him fast, before she caved to his touch all over again.

"We can see each other, Lexi, just not in such public forums. I might not be able to be at your side during your fancy black-ties, but I want to be in every other part of your life."

She shook her head, stinging from his unwitting rejection, but resolute. "That is my life."

Muffin entered the conversation, perhaps drawn by the sorrow in Lexi's voice. Lexi held her arms out to the dog, grateful for any barrier to erect between her and the man she wanted to be with.

"It's not your whole life, Lex. Why can't I be here to have cappuccino with you when you come home from those dinners?"

Unexpected tears welled. She wished she could be happy with just that much, but she'd never been a woman of half measures. Resenting the tears and the hurt, she adopted a tight smile. "Who says I come home after those events? Maybe that's when I like to hunt for my conquests."

Josh's brows lifted. "Then, how about I hang out with you during the week?" He patted Muffin on the head and shook her paw. "I can help you paint Muffin's nails."

Lexi stared down at the dog's bright red nails matching her own. The thought of big, burly Josh bent over Muffin's tiny black paw was more than she could bear.

"It wouldn't work."

"Because you won't let it?"

"Because I won't settle for a secret affair and avoiding the press in order to have a relationship." Although God knew, if anyone made her want to change her mind, it was the tough guy stretched out beside her.

He shook his head. "It wouldn't have to be like that. Lexi, it's not like I don't want to be with you. This is my job."

"It's about my job, too. And despite how superficial my fashion critiques look to the rest of the world, my life isn't about fashion. It's about holding an audience's attention with one topic long enough to make them hear messages about other topics they don't always want to hear."

She gained strength as she reiterated her mission, secure in the knowledge that—logically—she had chosen the right path for herself. Too bad it currently hurt like hell.

"I spent a lifetime being shushed by everyone around me. I'm not about to embark on any relationship I can't announce to the whole world." Anonymous sex was one thing. An anonymous relationship was another altogether.

He studied her, searched her soul with penetrating gray eyes.

"You're saying if I don't appear in public with you, then we don't have anything together?"

The lump in her throat wouldn't let her do more than nod.

He sat up, his gorgeous body bared to her gaze one final time.

"Woman, I thought I'd seen your best moves when you tossed me flat on my damn back tonight." He rubbed a hand across his chest. "But that's one hell of a follow-up punch you've got there."

Lexi might have argued the point, might have told him he hadn't exactly left her unscathed tonight, either. But for once her communication skills failed her. She had no words left to tell him how she felt, no hope of describing the ache in her heart as she watched him slide on his pants to leave.

11

HE'D OFFERED TO PAINT the dog's nails for chrissake.

Josh landed a left cross squarely on the gym's red leather punching bag, following it up with a flurry of quick blows that mirrored his frustration.

How the hell had he gone from self-sufficient New York police detective to sappy dog manicurist in the course of a weekend? Not that he really would have cared if only Lexi had said yes to him. But he'd gone and blown his best sensitive-guy routine for squat.

Zilch. Right hook.

Nada. Left uppercut.

Damn. He stilled the bag with sweaty arms, his breathing the lone sound in the otherwise empty workout room at the back of Marley's gym.

He'd thought Lexi would be a soft touch compared to the other women he'd dated. Not only did she color-coordinate her nails with her dogs', she also worked in a world of glittering sophistication. All of Josh's exes were either on the force or somehow associated with it—women every bit as tough as their jobs and their training.

He hadn't expected Lexi to be such a pit bull, given her china doll appearance. But she was tenacious about her career, serious as hell about her charity missions—and Josh found himself admiring her more than ever.

The sound of the bell on the gym's front door jarred him.

"Hey, Winger!" Rookie detective Otis Stanton strode into the gym, peeling off his sunglasses as he made his way toward the locker room. "I think that bag is getting the best of you, buddy. Maybe you'd better throw in the towel before this match turns ugly."

"The bag is tough, Stanton, but don't think I couldn't whip your butt inside of ten minutes." Who the hell were these rookie cops, anyway? What was this kid—all of nineteen?

Josh refused to think about the fact that Stanton was barely older than the wayward teen who'd shot down another cop last summer.

The junior baby looked nonplussed. In fact, the kid had the nerve to grin. "I'll stick to hitting the weights this week."

Good. The kid was obviously scared spitless.

Stanton paused as he unearthed tape from his gym bag. "The word at the station is there's a big shipment hitting New York this weekend—maybe in the Garment District. Is your team working on it?"

Josh started unlacing his boxing gloves, regretting his decision to stop at the gym before going to the precinct. Lexi was already messing with his control, affecting how he did his job. "How confirmed is this rumor?"

The kid shrugged, winding tape around his hands. "Pretty firm. I'm surprised they haven't—"

Josh's cell phone started ringing on cue.

"—called you already."

Tension rippling through him, Josh flipped open his phone with his freed hand. "Winger."

He prepped himself for hearing the latest word on a possible influx of drugs into the city. He wasn't prepared for the voice of one of the downtown research guys.

"Josh, it's Mikey. You wanted me to look up this Anton Bertrand."

His brain shifted gears as he tugged off his other glove with his teeth. Otis disappeared into the locker room, leaving Josh to get his head out of the clouds— or maybe out of Lexi Mansfield's apartment.

"I'm ready."

"At first look, there's nothing. These rich guys are aces at having their records mopped up."

"But eventually you found..." Normally Josh didn't mind the long version of the research process, but this case meant too much to him. For that matter, Lexi meant too much to him, to let Mikey waste any time getting to the point.

The junior guy huffed out a sigh. "Some juvenile brushes with the law including small-time drug dealing. Chances are he still knows some people in the business."

Or maybe he ran the business. "Thanks, Mike. Tomorrow morning that girly coffee you like is on me."

Mikey snorted. "It's a latte, Winger. Last time you wanted to reward me I had to choke my way through an espresso."

"Caffeine is caffeine to me. But I'll get it right this

time.'' Lexi would have known the difference. ''Tell the deputy inspector I'm looking into the big shipment hitting New York and I'll be in soon.''

But first he had a few other things to take care of. As he headed for the showers, Josh flipped open his phone to dial one more number.

He didn't need help keeping Lexi safe, but he owed it to Duke to clue him in to the situation—at least the PG-rated portions of the situation.

Lexi was in more trouble than he'd realized. Hell, the woman lived and breathed trouble. It might not faze her, but Josh wasn't taking any more chances. He needed to move her out of harm's way until he checked out the anonymous notes and followed this lead on Anton.

And if that meant he had to park himself on her doorstep—or in her velvet chaise longue—until she listened to reason, that was one sacrifice he was only too happy to make.

LEXI WAS DONE sacrificing her hopes and dreams for other people.

She repeated the words like an endless motivational tape in her mind as she trekked home from her morning outing to Neiman Marcus.

In the wake of Josh's defection, shopping hadn't held its usual allure. Instead of deriving pleasure from trying on gorgeous clothes, Lexi found herself wishing Josh could see her in the scarlet suede mini-dress, wondering what he'd think of the cute, pink-feather bustle-skirt, and envisioning how much the man would have drooled over the skintight leather boots that had been the day's shopping coup.

Of course, she was done sacrificing her hopes and dreams for other people.

She squeezed her eyes shut to impress the notion upon her brain as she juggled her bags up Broadway. She'd suppressed her own desires and squelched most of her irreverent thoughts while growing up in her parents' home. Lexi had been as foreign as an alien creature to her quiet, academic family. Although she'd always been confident of their love, she'd been aware of an underlying disapproval of her goal to conquer the fashion world.

What neither of her parents had ever realized was that Lexi had found a way to indulge her passion for fashion while fixing half the world's ills at the same time. Sure, she got to parade around in Versace dresses and Bill Blass gowns, but she raised boatloads of money for the homeless, sick and otherwise endangered because of her notable name and her broad media appeal.

Not a bad claim to fame for a middle-class girl with a Jersey accent.

And although Lexi wanted a man in her life one day, she'd been too busy and, frankly, too self-centered during the years that she built her career to have time for anyone else. And now...

Now she'd found the perfect guy without even looking, except that Josh Winger only wanted parts of her, and she wasn't willing to wholesale off parts of her personality to suit anyone.

Somehow, someway, she would find a man to embrace her outrageous sense of style, her runaway opinions, her Romanesque nose *and* her public persona, damn it.

She rounded the corner of Sixty-second Street just as the smell of smoke hit her.

The scene on the street confused her, disoriented her. A throng of maybe a hundred people stood in front of her building as other people streamed out. A thin trail of smoke seeped from the apartments, and as Lexi looked up at the twenty-story structure, she noticed the smoke seemed to be concentrated about midway up the building on the left front corner.

Right around her apartment.

Premonition, instinct, or maybe just plain old terror gripped her gut and twisted. She didn't need to count up the number of stories to know the fire was on the twelfth floor.

Muffin. She knew it wasn't right to worry about her dogs when there could be people in that building, but unfortunately, her dogs were the only faces she would recognize among the residents. She'd been so busy the past few years she hadn't even taken time to get to know her neighbors.

She ran down the street, heedless of the shopping bags banging her thighs, her sky-high heels, or the peep show she was giving in her miniskirt by pumping her legs like an Olympic runner. All those afternoons of track-and-field practice at boarding school were finally serving a purpose.

Skidding to a halt about a hundred yards from the door, Lexi stumbled into a crowd of onlookers. Sirens wailed in the distance, not nearly close enough for comfort.

She used the man's shoulders in front of her as leverage for a quick vertical leap. Even in her blasted high heels she could barely see the front door or what was going on. Damn.

The tall man turned as her feet hit the ground again. "They're evacuating the whole building for safety, but the fire's only on the twelfth floor right now."

Not waiting to hear any more, Lexi nudged the man aside and plowed her way through the crowd. If there was any way to get back inside and save Muffin, she needed to do it—now.

"Step aside! Twelfth-floor resident coming through." Lexi elbowed and pushed to the front of the throng, fear motivating her every step.

When she finally cleared the sea of onlookers and evacuees, Lexi found a clear view of the front door— and one lone straggler stumbling his way out of the building with a pack of yapping dogs at his feet.

Josh.

She squinted through the light haze of smoke, scarcely believing her eyes. But sure enough, dangerous Detective Winger currently juggled one gilded parakeet cage complete with squawking bird, one glass lemonade pitcher sloshing over with water and a bright pink beta fish, and a stack of picture frames jammed under his arm. Muffin, Harry and Snowball ran ahead of him, minus leashes.

Lexi dropped her Neiman Marcus bags and launched herself toward Josh, singing a litany of "Ohmigod, ohmigod, ohmigod."

The dogs saw her first and ran to greet her, their barks almost as loud as the nearing fire engine siren. She couldn't think about them yet, however, not until she'd thanked Josh.

Lexi pried the lemonade pitcher out of his arms, her heart clenching at the sight of the soot on his once-white dress shirt. "Are you okay?"

She set the pitcher down on the sidewalk and turned to wrench away the small stack of framed photographs he must have grabbed from her nightstand— Lexi's parents at their wedding, Lexi's great-grandparents at Ellis Island, a family reunion in Capri when she was just a toddler.

Josh grinned, his teeth brilliantly white against skin slightly grayed skin from ash in the fire. "Never better."

He set down the parakeet cage to rampant applause from the crowd at the base of the apartment building. For a man who didn't like the spotlight, he sure did a good job of putting himself smack-dab in the middle of it.

The dogs were already being patted, stroked and soothed by kind strangers united in crisis on West Sixty-second Street. People smiled at her and Josh, maybe encouraged by Josh's triumphant exit.

The need to fling herself into his arms almost overwhelmed her, but she stomped it down and settled for letting him turn her heart to mush as he whistled a comforting little tune to her bird.

She tucked a few strands of curly hair behind her ear to keep her hands busy, to keep herself from touching every part of her hero. "How did you know about the fire?"

As the fire engines pulled up to the curb, Josh moved their menagerie along with the rest of the crowd to the back of the sidewalk.

"I didn't. I came over here to move you someplace safe until I get to the bottom of the anonymous notes." He wiped a hand across his forehead.

Only then did Lexi notice the beads of sweat cooling on his temple. Good God, he'd walked right into a burning apartment for her animals. For her.

"You think the note writer did this?" The notion shocked her. She'd dismissed the notes as a creepy way to scare her, but she'd never thought the writer would take action against her.

"Probably. I think you're posing a bigger threat than we realized with your articles. Either way, I want you out of here."

Lexi stared up at the burning twelfth floor. "I don't think I'll have a choice but to leave now."

She was pretty sure her voice didn't quiver when she said it, but Josh must have known she was scared out of her mind anyway because he backed her into his chest, wrapped his arms around her and squeezed.

Together, they watched the firefighters run into the building in full gear.

Josh bent close enough to whisper in her ear. "Someone set the fire in your apartment, Lexi. It was the only one burning when I got up there."

If her blood hadn't run cold enough to start with, it had just turned arctic.

"You're sure?" Who could hate her enough to do

this? And how could her fashion commentary threaten someone enough to drive them to arson?

"Positive. The fire department will have the blaze controlled pretty easily, but your apartment is going to be unlivable. Duke told me you have a key to get into Amanda's loft?"

She nodded, resigning herself to the plan but unable to get her feet in gear yet, her eyes lingering on the smoking building.

"We really ought to go, Lexi, in case whoever set the fire is still hanging around." Josh picked up her shopping bags and the birdcage as he glanced up and down the street.

She moved to grab the lemonade pitcher that poor Bubblegum was using as a temporary fish tank when a woman standing behind her tugged on Lexi's sleeve. "Excuse me, miss, but your dog seems determined to hang on to something."

Only then did Lexi take a good look at her babies. Muffin and Snowball basked in the glory of their last-minute escape, tails wagging in the contentment of the crowd's attention.

Harry, however, sat at attention. He looked up at Lexi, jaw clenched, a small chunk of something red clamped between his teeth.

Lexi knelt to his level. "What is it, boy? Do you have something for Mommy?" Only when she stroked his head and gently pulled on the red object did Harry let it go.

"What is it?" Josh leaned over her shoulder, squinting to see the small red swatch.

"Fabric. Very wet, dog-drooled fabric." Lexi

turned the square-inch piece over in her hand. "Make that dog-drooled cashmere, which makes a big difference. This is definitely nothing that came from inside my apartment."

"I'll take it to the lab to run some tests. Maybe Harry got in a fight with whoever set the fire." Josh nudged her gently forward. "But right now we'd better get out of here."

Lexi half heard him and took a step forward, but last year's fall collections kept playing over in her mind. Someone had used red cashmere like this, and the name of the designer teased the edges of her brain.

"In just a minute," she replied absently, mentally rewinding all the fall runway shows. If only she could remember who designed it, maybe she could find out who owned it.

"Lexi, I mean it. We need to hit the road if we want to—"

Lexi looked up as his words trailed off. She followed his gaze across the crowded street to the white sport utility vehicle with a "TV 11" logo in bright blue emblazoned on the side.

"If we want to avoid the media?" she supplied, knowing exactly why Josh was in such a rush to get out of there.

The look he sent her would have frozen a normal woman to the spot. "And if we want to keep you alive to write next week's column."

Lexi shook her head, hoping a little levity would cover the hurt she felt inside at the thought that he would never want to be seen with her. "I wouldn't dream of dying on you, Josh. Can you imagine the negative publicity?"

"Actually, I can."

He whistled for the dogs and scooped up Bubble-gum's container, effectively leaving her with nothing to carry. He stomped down the street toward his car, which she could see parked half a block behind the fire trucks.

"You can?"

"The last person I was looking out for I ended up shooting, Lexi."

That stopped her in her shoes. "You're kidding."

Josh seemed to be cursing himself under his breath as he set down Lexi's things and fished for his keys in his pants pocket. "Extra, extra, you can read all about it if you want. It was in every paper in the city a few months ago."

As he opened the door to his car, Lexi's dogs couldn't scramble into his back seat fast enough.

Why hadn't Amanda mentioned this event to her? Wouldn't Duke have been upset if his partner had truly hurt somebody? Her mind refused to picture Josh shooting someone without damn good cause. "I was in Europe a lot this summer—why don't you refresh me?"

Josh loaded her pictures in the back seat of his unmarked cop car. "Hop in, I'll tell you."

She stepped closer to the vee of the car's open door, creating a semi-intimate setting despite the throng of people milling half a block away. "Tell me now or I'm going nowhere."

She should be scared, shouldn't she? A dangerous-looking cop confesses to shooting someone in his custody.

But she wasn't. Lexi could see beyond the glower to the regret in Josh's eyes.

He half sighed, half growled out his frustration. "I had been sort of working with a city informant in a drug case, when the kid decided it wasn't enough to turn evidence against the buddies who had wronged him—he wanted revenge, instead."

Her whole body tensed. "What happened?"

"The kid showed up at the scene of a drug bust one night and went wild." Josh clenched his jaw a few times in quick succession. "He hit and killed one of the traffickers before a cop noticed him and turned a gun to him. The kid shot the cop and I shot the kid. End of story."

"Not end of story." No matter how much he might think otherwise, Josh needed to talk about this as much as she needed—wanted—to hear it. "How young a kid are we talking about?"

"Sixteen." Frustration laced the word. He tilted his head back to stare up at the sky for a moment. "Lex, I'm sorry I'm trying to hustle you out of here, but we really should go."

She smoothed her fingers along his shirtsleeve, keeping her touch featherlight. "Did he die?"

He brushed some ash off his clothes. "The kid, yes. The cop, no. But the cop wouldn't have gone down in the first place if I'd done a better job with the kid. I had been talking to him, you know? Trying to bring him around to life without crime. Piss-poor decision."

The narrow look he shot her declared the topic

closed. He pulled Lexi around to the other side of the car and held the front door for her. "Now get in the car, we're going."

"That's why you don't like the media?" Call her clueless, but Josh offered up so precious little about himself, she wanted to be sure she got it right.

"I have no problem with the media," he clarified, his tight smile looking close to a grimace. "But as an occasional undercover guy, I need to stay out of the papers for the next year or so until all that dies down. Then I can go back to hitting some heavy-duty undercover assignments."

She really wanted to know why he liked working undercover more than he liked her. Couldn't he choose to work undercover with her and outside the damn covers at work?

But she didn't have a chance to ask another question, because he slammed her car door shut with a bit more force than was strictly necessary.

Curse the man.

He'd saved her dogs, her parakeet and even her pink fish, and in the course of an afternoon, Josh had made her realize their relationship was built on far more than sex.

Too bad Josh didn't seem to realize it.

After hearing about Josh's stint in the public eye, Lexi understood things weren't as cut-and-dried with him as she'd first thought. He was a man with as much heart as muscle, judging by how torn up he'd been at the memory of a dead criminal. He was a complex man with intriguing layers.

And for some reason, Lexi couldn't help but envision how rewarding it would be to personally uncover every one of those delectable layers.

JOSH PULLED UP to the famous Matthews design showroom in the Garment District a few minutes later. Amanda Matthews still kept a loft apartment above the showroom, a space Duke said she was slowly converting into her own design studio.

As Josh scoped out the parking situation, he spotted a familiar red Harley-Davidson in front of the showroom's display window. The time of reckoning drew near, now that Rawlins was back in town. Josh wondered if Duke would believe his relationship with Lexi was based on more than sex.

It worked against Josh that he hadn't had many relationships based on more than sex in the past decade. But that wasn't because he hadn't been openminded. He just hadn't found a woman who really held his attention long term.

His work had always been completely absorbing. Okay, and maybe a part of him didn't want to commit the same failings as his parents. No kid of his would be shuffled into the middle of a fierce divorce just because he didn't know his own mind.

Josh had always told himself he wouldn't bother initiating a long-term relationship unless he found someone who genuinely fascinated him. And frankly, Lexi did.

"Looks like they beat us back," Lexi noted, eyeing the motorcycle. "You think Duke is going to blow a gasket about us seeing each other? He does sort of think of me as the baby sister for some reason."

"Duke's usually pretty reasonable." He hoped. He slung his arm over the steering wheel to keep from touching Lexi. That long, wild hair of hers had a way of drawing his touch. "But I don't think either of them is going to appreciate knowing about the one-night stand."

"Technically a two-night stand in our case."

"Right. I think they'd be fine if we were pursuing a serious relationship, but since you aren't ready to—"

"You mean since *you* aren't ready to, Mr. Camera Shy."

"I vote we keep our mouths shut about the whole thing and fake like we met yesterday when Duke asked me to check up on you."

Lexi flashed him a thumbs-up sign far too quickly for his taste. Couldn't she at least consider his suggested arrangement for seeing each other?

But she was already climbing out of the car with her dogs in tow. They followed her up the street like ducks in a row, each knowing his or her place in the pecking order behind the fashion princess. God, she was a sight to see. While she wasn't exactly beautiful in Hollywood terms, she was a woman you couldn't ignore.

Heads turned and gossip flowed wherever Lexi went.

Damn, but she was so wrong for him. Why did he have to want her so much anyway?

Josh sprinted to catch up to her. "Honey, you can't just take off on me like that. You're officially in danger now, so you can't strut the streets of New York like you own them.''

She dug in her purse for her keys, setting off for him a sexual stream of consciousness—purse, leopard-spotted purse, leopard panties, scintillating sex.

This was going to be a long night.

''Sorry.'' She let them into the famous design showroom full of luxurious clothes, marble floors and faceless mannequins, then led them through the store to the stairs in the back. ''I guess I'm going to have to think through my actions a little bit more. I'm not used to staying out of the spotlight,'' she said as they climbed to the loft.

The tiny quaver in her voice did him in. Pausing just outside the door, Josh turned her toward him, needing her to listen.

''I'll keep you safe.'' His fingers pressed into the soft flesh of her arms, the delicate line of her shoulders. ''I promise.''

''I want to be safe from the rest of the world.'' Her keys jingled, forgotten in her constantly moving hands. ''Just not with you.''

The rattling keys faded to the background for him, too, as her words sank into his brain and the implication sank into his libido. ''You don't want to feel safe with me?''

The stairwell seemed to shrink in size, closing in around them to four private walls.

''I want to be adventurous and not hide away from the world.''

Ah. She was talking about something else entirely.

She was talking about his refusal to enter the limelight with her.

Too bad her proximity and that damn exotic scent of hers wouldn't let him concentrate on an intelligent answer. "Adventure I can give you, Lexi."

Her pouty lips said his form of adventure wouldn't be enough for her—a challenge his own mouth found too hard to resist.

He tipped her head back, the need to taste her so fierce he couldn't have walked away if he'd been in the path of an oncoming freight train. Just one taste...

His lips met hers and promptly incinerated the "just one taste" theory. Her scent hit his senses and flowed through him like good wine. And she didn't hold herself back from him, despite everything she'd spouted about them not having anything together now. No, Lexi plastered herself to him with as much enthusiasm as he pressed her into him.

She was all smooth curves and legs. Her mini-dress gave him access to her thighs, and for one crazy moment, he palmed her thigh and squeezed.

He wanted more than she should give him. Hell, he wanted everything she had.

But the timing didn't seem right when the door to Amanda's loft flew open.

Duke Rawlins stood there with his soon-to-be bride, Amanda. They held hands, and wore identical expressions of shock.

Josh tugged Lexi's skirt into place. Not that she'd really been showing anything crucial, but he needed to extricate his hand from underneath her dress, at least.

Not good.

Lexi gave herself a little wriggle and seemed to put everything back into position. "Hi, guys. Welcome home."

Her dogs backed up her friendly sentiment from behind them on the stairwell.

Duke didn't sound quite as chipper, however, when he leaned forward to point a threatening finger in Josh's face. "You'd better have earned your goddamn gynecology degree while I wasn't looking, Columbo, or else I ought to be hearing wedding bells ringing any freaking minute."

12

MEN.

Having grown up without the benefit of a brother, and having proceeded through most of her life without any sort of significant other, Lexi had to admit it was sort of fun to have two impossibly sexy guys in each other's faces because of her.

Juvenile? Definitely. But she'd missed out on moments like this at an all-girls boarding school, so maybe she could be excused for the high school thrill she felt for a couple of seconds.

Duke Rawlins looked like the Hollywood version of a New York City Police officer. He had a square jaw with a perfectly centered cleft in his chin and the same blue eyes that had made a whole generation of women weep over Frank Sinatra. Even Duke's black motorcycle jacket couldn't dim the effect of his spiky blond hair and baby blues.

He was no Josh Winger, of course. But then, Lexi always did go for the rebels.

As her grown-up instincts kicked in, she sidled in between the snarling big dogs.

"Thank you, Duke, but I'd prefer you keep me and *gynecology* out of the same sentence in the future." When Duke and Josh continued to lock narrowed eyes in some sort of testosterone-induced pissing match, she sent an SOS look to Amanda for reinforcement.

The glare worked, startling Amanda out of her shocked silence.

"And as for wedding bells, I think that's a bit premature, given that Lexi and Josh have only just started seeing each other." She looked to Lexi for confirmation of the fact.

Lexi felt a big eye-roll coming on, but stifled the impulse. "I guess you could say that." She leaned over to pick up Muffin, hoping her dog would at least prove an effective ally.

Before she had the chance to find out, however, Josh took a step forward, still eyeing Duke. "Maybe you ought to worry less about Lexi's personal life and more about who set her apartment on fire today."

The man had all the tact of a bulldog.

"Nice going, Winger," Lexi muttered, as Amanda paled five shades and Duke had to bolster her up. Lexi swatted Josh's shoulder with Muffin's paw for lack of better retaliation.

"Are you okay?" Amanda asked, shaking off her burly protector to pull Lexi forward into the loft full of fabric bolts and towering piles of swatch books.

"Who the hell did it?" Duke asked at the same time, his disgruntled big brother act forgotten in his haste to get information.

"I don't know, but we're sure as hell not going to find out with you breathing down my neck like an overeager rookie."

They grumbled at each other even as Duke helped Josh bring in Lexi's shopping bags and animals, leaving Lexi and Amanda to talk somewhat privately in the living room. Amanda poured water for all the dogs, poured wine for Lexi and tossed sunflower seeds in the parakeet's cage, firing questions all the while.

"Were you there when the fire started?" Amanda prodded, finally taking a seat on the arm of the sofa as the men debated where to hang the birdcage on the other side of the studio. "How much burned? Was Josh there with you?"

"I wasn't there." Lexi sipped her wine and stole glances at Josh over in the corner talking to Duke. "I guess Josh had come over to check on me and found the place burning up. He got all the animals out. And some pictures." Her eyes burned as she remembered seeing Josh balancing her fish and her bird.

Amanda cleared away a pile of fabric swatches from the steamer trunk that served as a coffee table and settled herself on the sturdy chest. "Are you okay, Lex? You know you can stay here as long as you want. I practically live at Duke's, anyway."

"I'm fine." She'd be better if Josh was sitting next to her. "And thank you. I would appreciate using the loft for a few weeks. I know where you keep everything here."

Amanda frowned. "You seem far too calm. Maybe you're in shock."

"Maybe." Or maybe she just couldn't take her eyes off Josh in his ashen clothes. Even the diamond stud in his ear was dulled from the coat of soot he still wore.

Oh God, she was totally falling for a cranky cop who wanted no part of her public world.

Amanda's gaze narrowed. "You're wild for Duke's partner, aren't you."

"He's completely yummy."

Amanda smothered a snort. "Are we talking about Joshua Winger? The guy that looks more criminal than cop?"

Lexi squinted her eyes, trying to see Josh objectively. "The guy with shoulders so damn straight God must have laid down a level to mold him? The guy with a tush any red-blooded woman would give her right eye to squeeze?"

Amanda tilted her head to the side, still staring at Josh.

Lexi knew the exact moment her friend understood what she was saying. A naughty little grin spread across the Revlon girl's features.

"Okay, quit ogling, girlfriend. You see my point."

"He *is* kind of cute."

"No. Muffin is 'cute.' That man is devastatingly sexy." Lexi watched as Duke paced and Josh talked on his cell phone. Harry the terrier fit right in on the guy's side of the room, standing at attention between the men.

"You met him because Duke asked him to check on you yesterday and he's already got his hand up your skirt?" Amanda snapped her fingers for Snowball, providing permission for the little shih tzu to jump on her lap.

"No. I met him because I handcuffed him at the Shelter the Homeless event." Come to think of it, she wouldn't mind having a pair of handcuffs at her disposal right now.

"You didn't."

"I most certainly did."

Amanda bit her lip. "He was probably trying not to stand out in the crowd, Lexi. He went there to work."

"How does a man like that blend in, may I ask you? I noticed him from at least fifty yards away in a room packed with nearly five hundred people."

Amanda might have answered, but they noticed Duke charging over toward their corner of the loft. They sipped their wine and pretended they hadn't just been whispering about the guys.

Duke strode in between the sofas. "Sorry to interrupt, ladies, but we need to follow up on this fire and a couple of other things." His gaze turned to Amanda. "I'll meet you back at my place tonight?"

Amanda practically purred. "Rooftop rendezvous at midnight. Don't be late."

Their shared liplock wasn't any hotter than the kisses Lexi had been sharing with Josh all weekend. But damn it, Amanda and Duke had forever to kiss like that.

Once Josh had caught his bad guys, Lexi wouldn't even see him.

She glanced toward him, only to find those gray eyes studying her, assessing her. A wave of heat jumped across the room as their gazes connected. Joined.

He was the first to speak. "I need that red swatch

Harry found. The lab is going to run some tests on it.''

So maybe she was the only one feeling heat waves. Damn the man.

She dug in her purse and came up with the still-damp cashmere. ''I remember who used this. It was from a Valentino collection last year.''

Josh frowned. ''Valentino who? Does this guy have any reason to want to scare you?''

''He's a designer, Columbo,'' Duke intervened as he stepped away from Amanda. ''He must have made the threads Harry found.''

Amanda snapped her fingers. ''I remember that collection. I bet we could contact their showroom to at least find out a few of the customers who would have bought any of the red cashmere.''

''I'll call right now.'' Lexi reached for her purse and the electronic organizer it contained.

Josh grabbed her wrist before she could get there. ''Not this time, Lex. You're too damn involved in this already. I don't want you getting yourself in any deeper.''

''But I've got the number right here.''

''Give it to me and I'll call.'' His brows practically glued themselves together, he was frowning so hard.

''Fine.'' She pressed some numbers into her address book program and wrote the information down on a sticky note. Now Mr. Undercover wouldn't even let her help figure out who torched her apartment.

She slapped the paper into his hand with a bit too much force.

Josh squeezed her hand into his. "You okay, Lexi?"

"Peachy. Why don't you go solve the world's crimes while I wait here and file my nails?" He really didn't get it, did he? Couldn't he see she wanted to be with him, wanted to help him work on his case and be a part of things that were important to him?

Then she chided herself. Of course he couldn't. He didn't want her to be a part of his world any more than he wanted to be a part of hers.

He could only see Lexi the glamorous bad girl. He didn't know anything about the rest of her.

Josh sent her one of those glares that would have made a normal woman cry. "You know, it wouldn't hurt for you to be marginally scared, Lex. There's such a thing as a healthy dose of fear."

Despite the hellish day she'd just had, Lexi was only scared of one thing right now. And that was not seeing Josh again once he walked out that door.

He wouldn't be back. Not since she'd turned him down along with his offer for a partial relationship. Their kiss on the stairs to the loft had been just a knee-jerk reaction to the fire, the adrenaline rush in the aftermath of fear.

Stifling the impulse to pull him into her arms and not let go, she blew him a kiss and waggled her fingers in an exaggerated wave. "'Bye, tiger. Don't worry about me. Harry seems to like his new protector role."

She pretty much expected him to slam the door on his way out.

But she hadn't been counting on the echoing emptiness he'd leave in his wake.

SLAMMING THE DOOR didn't come close to satisfying the anger churning through Josh as he stomped down the stairs of Amanda's loft with Duke.

"You hear that? She'll let the damn dog protect her instead of me. How the hell do you like that for an endorsement?"

Duke whistled low under his breath as they hit the street. Night had fallen, knocking down the temperature a few degrees. "She's tougher than she looks, I'll give you that. I remember Amanda telling me once that her money is always on Lexi in a fight."

"Does that mean she frequently rips out hearts for fun?" How could she just wave him away tonight, after the kind of day she'd had? After the weekend they'd had? Josh considered himself a stiff-upper-lip kind of guy, but he was a tied-in-knots damn wreck just knowing someone was out to hurt Lexi.

"You've got it that bad, man?"

"No." Josh wanted that clarified right now. Lexi didn't have any intention of having a relationship with him unless he yelled it from a damn mountaintop. And he couldn't—wouldn't—do that right now. "Any man that wants Lexi has to take on a whole lifestyle—it'd be like running for mayor. You know I can't afford to put myself out in the public eye like that. Not in this line of work."

Sliding into the car, Josh tossed the police light in the front window and turned it on.

"So don't go undercover anymore. You've been

out there enough to know you can only do it so long. One of these days you'll be fingered for a fake."

"Me? With this face? I blend in pretty well with the bad guys, remember?" Josh pulled into traffic and hit the gas, hard. He needed to get to the station and talk to about fifty different people to make sense of this case—starting with the fire department.

"Undercover work has a shelf life, Josh. Don't tell me you don't know that as well as I do." Duke held on to the dashboard as Josh careened around a corner.

"That's crap. You're working this angle just because you've got some new morality since you met Amanda." He forced himself to concentrate on the road and not Duke's silver-tongued maneuvering. "You said it yourself—you expect to hear cursed wedding bells. Well, it's not going to happen."

"Scared shitless, aren't you, Winger?" Duke flashed him his Hollywood grin as they reached the Tenth Precinct and parked the car out front.

"She owns a poodle for chrissake. Why the hell would I be scared?"

"Seems to me I've never seen you turn on the police light to get back to the station."

Josh told him exactly where he could stick his Oprah psychobabble as he slammed the car door.

Lexi Mansfield might have drop-dead legs and a killer smile, but that didn't scare Josh. Hell, no.

Maybe it made him a little sexually frustrated when he couldn't be with her every minute of the day. And a little freaked out that someone would try to hurt her.

But that did not make him scared of falling for her

smart mouth or her wicked ways in bed. And he would prove it just as soon as he sewed up this case, because he'd be walking away from Lexi for good.

That's the way she wanted it, damn it, and that's the way it would be.

NEARLY A WEEK after the fire, Amanda stopped by the loft to bring Lexi more clothes and to torture her with questions about Josh.

The week had crawled by without the sexy detective to liven things up. He'd politely called her three times, but each time he had limited conversation to the arson and smuggling investigations. He'd also dutifully stationed a plainclothes cop in a car on the street to keep a watch on her, but Josh had yet to make an appearance. He'd keep her safe, but he wouldn't come near her.

Not that she could blame him, after she'd given him his marching orders in no uncertain terms last weekend. But she didn't want to trot out her heartache right now, not when she had a big charity event to get ready for tonight. Time to forget about Josh and get back to her real life.

Lexi kept digging through the matching leather designer suitcases, ostensibly to check out the new offerings Amanda had brought, but really she just wanted to hide from conversation about the man who had turned her life upside down for one wild weekend and then all but disappeared from her life.

"So he still hasn't stopped by?" Amanda asked for what seemed like the tenth time as she rifled around the loft for hangers.

"He's called to check on me." Lexi sidestepped the question to avoid seeming pathetic. "Wow, Amanda, you didn't have to bring over stuff from your new fall collection." She held up a pencil-thin mermaid gown with aqua-colored sequins curling up the front like undulating seaweed.

Amanda's cheeks went just a little pink. "Um, that's sort of self-serving, actually, because I'm hoping you'll opt to wear it for the Dance for Children."

"Of course I will wear it!" Lexi hopped off the couch to hug her best friend. "I would be honored to wear one of your designs. If anything, I try hard not to brag on you too much in my column."

"You are wonderfully diplomatic." Amanda pulled a black scarf out of the suitcase and tied it around Lexi's neck, falling into the dress-up games they'd been playing together ever since boarding school. "And I figured this way, you don't even need to mention me in your column. Just the dress on your body will make the pages of six different publications and flood my phone with orders for a month." She adjusted the knot in Lexi's scarf and nodded her satisfaction.

"You shrewd businessperson, you." Lexi peered in a three-panel mirror Amanda kept stashed behind a sewing machine. Inspired by the fifties look of the scarf, she pulled a rubber band out of her purse and tied her hair in a ponytail.

"Flattery will not make me forget what we were discussing, however." Amanda started filling one of the loft's umpteen rolling racks with a temporary wardrobe for Lexi. "Why hasn't Josh been over here?

After that kiss I saw him giving you last week, I assumed you two were pretty hot and heavy.''

''I lured him home for a one-night stand that turned into a two-night stand, but we're mature enough to know that's where it ends.''

''You brought him to *your* home?'' Amanda gaped at her, a pink satin bustier dangling in midair from her fingers.

Leave it to Amanda to cue in on that unusual fact.

''His house was being painted.'' Lexi continued to hand her clothes to try to nudge her off the subject.

''You told me once that you would never bring any guy but the 'right' guy into your private sanctuary.''

Had she said that? ''I guess I underestimated the sexual appeal of men like Josh Winger.''

''Uh-huh.'' Amanda went back to work, hanging two Chanel suits. ''And what makes you think you're not meant to be together?''

Knowing Amanda wouldn't give up this line of questioning anytime soon, Lexi offered the abbreviated version. ''Josh doesn't want to be a part of my lifestyle. I'm too public for him because of his job or something.''

''It's as simple as that?''

Lexi shrugged, toying with the tiny buttons on a green silk nightgown with the tags still attached. ''He would hate my kind of publicity, anyway. You know I still get lots of jibes about my total lack of blue blood. He might resent being lumped with me as the mule in thoroughbred finery, you know? I don't give a flying fig what people say about me, but I wouldn't want anyone to slander Josh.''

Amanda tossed a suitcase full of shoes on the floor and sat down on the sofa next to Lexi. "Do you love him?"

"I only just met him."

"Question still stands."

Lexi tried to consider the idea rationally. Was there a rational side of her left where Josh was concerned?

"Maybe. Probably. But how do I know?" She stared down at the green nightgown and tried to picture Josh's reaction to it. Very, very enticing. "We spent two amazing nights together. I'm probably just horribly naive to think I'm in love with him."

"You'll know for sure when it happens." Amanda looked out the windows of the loft, surely remembering another time, another declaration of love.

Lexi envied her, envied that moment.

"But in the meantime, it's my duty as a friend to remind you that anyone and everyone in the public eye has had negative publicity. Maybe you receive more than your share, but that's just because you are flamboyant."

"You still think that crocheted dress I wore to your store's grand opening was over the top, don't you."

Amanda couldn't hide her grin. She opened a train case to reveal a pile of gloves, pins, hair accessories and little purses. "I wouldn't have worn a miniature tablecloth in public, but that's just me. Face it, Lex, you thrive on controversy in your public life. It gets you more ink and more attention for your causes."

"True. But Josh would have hated that." Those strong, silent types didn't understand the subtle rises and falls of media figures. Josh would think it was petty and superficial.

Amanda dug a silk flower out of the train case and tucked the red bloom behind Lexi's ear. "No, he would admire you for the way you manipulate money from deep pockets into charitable hands, the same way all your friends do. Regardless of where you came from or what you choose to wear to any grand opening, you'll always have more class in your little finger than Simone Bertrand has in her whole liposucked body."

The doorbell rang before Lexi had the chance to bawl her eyes out at Amanda's generous words. She patted the red flower in her hair as she walked to the door.

"I hope you're right, Amanda, that my claim to class resides in my little finger and not this hair." As she opened the front door, she tugged at the long mane she'd tied up in a ponytail.

Amanda frowned as the team of stylists in white salon uniforms strode into the loft's living area. "What do you mean? Or should I be afraid to ask?"

"You know the old song about washing that man right out of your hair? I'm going to cut mine right out of my hair and donate the whole black mess to those places that make wigs for kids who've undergone chemo." Lexi allowed the lead stylist, a hairdresser named Bruno, to guide her into a chair near one of the floor-to-ceiling windows.

"That's so sweet!" Amanda straightened a pair of metal-studded pumps beneath a rolling rack, then joined the styling team as they circled Lexi's chair.

She wheeled the three-panel mirror over so Lexi could keep tabs on the situation.

"I'm going to give the hair to the people at Dance for Children tonight." She hoped she liked shoulder-length hair. Her curls had hit her waist for as long as she could remember. "You think it'll work to make me forget Josh?"

Amanda walked around behind Lexi's chair, clamped her hands on her friend's shoulders and leaned forward until both their faces were visible in the mirror. "Not a chance."

No kidding. Lexi was probably just as apt to forget to breathe.

13

JOSH STRAIGHTENED HIS TIE in the alley behind Club Blue, New York's hot spot of the month located in a long-neglected storefront in midtown. Limousines mobbed the street in front of the club, but a red carpet entrance wasn't exactly Josh's style. He flashed a badge at the security guy guarding the back door and quietly slipped inside Lexi's gala Dance for Children event.

He hadn't meant to come here tonight. He could think of ten reasons he ought to stay away from Lexi. Hell, he'd been reciting those reasons all week in an effort not to darken her doorstep at the loft.

But he couldn't leave her security to the plainclothes guy who'd been assigned to watch her. Not in this crowd. Besides, having been hunted down by Lexi at a club like this the week before, Josh knew firsthand that the woman moved like quicksilver through a crowd. He was willing to bet she could elude a rookie without lifting a manicured nail to try.

"Can I get you a drink, sir?" A waitress emerged from the black-tie crowd. Unlike the waitresses at last week's club who had worn slinky togas, the waitresses at Club Blue wore elegant dresses the color of the sea. The impatient woman in front of him twitched from foot to foot in hers. "Well?"

Josh scanned the scene for glimpses of Lexi, but came up blank. "I'd like to send a mai tai to Lexi Mansfield, the event hostess. Do you know who I mean?"

The woman's mouth gaped with insult, sort of like Lexi's fish, Bubblegum. "Every woman in New York knows Lexi Mansfield." The waitress narrowed her eyes. "Do you know her?"

Josh flipped a bill on the woman's drink tray. "She asked to meet me here. Could you point her out before you deliver the drink? I'm having a hell of a time locating anyone in this crowd."

He was also having a hell of a time waiting to see Lexi. The week had crawled by like a never-damn-ending eternity, given that he was dreaming about her every night and fantasizing about her every day.

The waitress pocketed the tip and pointed to a stately older guy in a tuxedo and a sexy sylph in turquoise sequins who were waltzing their way across the dance floor to a disco beat.

Josh recognized Jeeves—or was it James?—the classy butler from Simone Bertrand's Long Island mansion. But while the butler's dance partner was certainly recognizable, she was also missing two feet of wild black hair.

Lexi had cut off her hair? Josh gaped in surprise, not because she didn't look gorgeous, but because most women who grew their hair as long as Lexi's usually seemed pretty attached to their manes.

He indulged the urge to stare at her unseen in the

shadows of the club. She danced the same way she moved through life, in constant, effortless motion. Her shorter hair just brushed her shoulders, leaving an enticing expanse of skin bared to his gaze.

Damn lucky for Jeeves that he wasn't touching any of that bare skin. Not so damn lucky for the plainclothes guy who was supposed to be protecting Lexi. Josh didn't see the cop anywhere in sight.

He barreled through the crowd to get to her, telling himself he was in such a hurry because she could be in danger, knowing the real reason probably had more to do with the fact that he hadn't touched her in almost a week.

Reaching the dance floor in record time, Josh tapped the butler on the shoulder. He forced a polite "May I?" out of his mouth, although the Neanderthal in him screamed something more along the line of "Out of my way, she's taken."

But even Josh couldn't snarl at a guy who snapped an old-school bow to Lexi and kissed her hand like he was Cary Grant.

After the butler disappeared into the well-heeled crush, nothing impeded Josh's view of Lexi. And what a view.

She smiled that wicked grin. The one that made him remember every illicit moment they'd spent together in vivid detail.

"Cat got your tongue?"

Only then did Josh realize he was single-handedly creating a scene, standing there ogling her in the middle of the packed dance floor.

"Maybe my tongue is just conserving its strength

for later." He took her arm and tugged her off the dance floor, seized by uncharacteristic impulsiveness.

Her skin was so smooth, so cool. Josh wondered how fast he could take her temperature up a few degrees if he could find someplace private.

"Maybe your tongue would be better off for the exercise," Lexi grumbled, although she quickly assumed a smile for the waitress who brought her mai tai. Lexi sipped at it steadily as she followed him across the bar to the cloakroom.

Josh flashed his badge at the attendant and tipped her generously, but he secured the room and some time alone for a few minutes at least. Jackets, capes and shawls of all kinds lined the walls and were piled high on a table in the middle of the small space. A mixture of perfume scents wafted from the coats, surrounding them in a fog of flowers, musk and maybe some Chanel Number Five.

He yanked down the screen over the counter to enhance their privacy, but the thumping music from the club still rocked the walls.

"Are you complaining about how I use my tongue, Lexi?" He knew he had no right to touch her, but his hands found their way to her hips anyhow. Sequins bit into his palms, but his fingers rested on the satiny skin of her back.

She stared up at him with dark, gypsy eyes, her exotic scent wrapping around him, distinguishing itself from the hundred other perfumes in the room.

"I'm limiting my complaints to your conversational skills." Her voice was breathy, but she slid herself out of his grip, anyway, stationing herself near a rack of lightweight overcoats and delicate shawls. "But they really do need improvement. Care to tell me why you're here, after you specifically turned down the offer to be my guest?"

"I'm doing my job."

"Your job involves titillating conversation and a clandestine rendezvous in the coatroom?" She cocked her head to one side, her hands planted on her hips.

Her nails shone opalescent in the dim light: pink nails decorated with silver fish.

Damn, but she was a trip. A sexy-as-hell, take-no-lip trip.

"No, Lex. My job involves checking up on my rookie cops who don't know better than to leave you to your own devices in this building full of sharks. I don't know who's supposed to be watching you, but I am so going to kick his ass."

She unfolded her arms and paced the tiny space, her shorter hair bouncing behind her in a dance of spiral curls. "Maybe your job ought to involve telling these guys that if they're going to watch me on my turf, they need to wear a tie to a black-tie event. I sent Otis off on a mission to pick up something more suitable."

Otis had left her by herself? Josh's buddy from the gym was going to get treated to a one-on-one boxing lesson next week.

"The guy's a cop, not a clotheshorse, Lexi. What were you thinking?" He moved closer to her, needing to impress his message on her somehow. "Do you realize how vulnerable you are here? Especially given the fact that it's probably one of your uptown fashion friends who is burning down apartments and turning wayward kids into bonafide criminals?''

Lexi reached up to smooth his tie. The simple gesture—a domestic staple that probably wouldn't mean much to a guy who'd grown up among family—touched him in a way he didn't even begin to understand.

"Too bad other cops aren't like you, Josh. The average detective doesn't know how to navigate the waters of New York society."

"That's ludicrous, Lexi. You know I have no idea what I'm doing around these people. Hell, I can't even talk to you in front of all those highbrows, so I just spent half my paycheck to buy off the coat-check girl."

"See? You got what you wanted without offending the social matrons by kissing me senseless on the dance floor. You manage to fit even where you don't fit." She slid her fingers down the lapels of his jacket, raked her eyes over his chest. "We're sort of alike in that way."

"Lady, if you think I've got what I want, you're sadly mistaken." Still, he had to admit he sort of liked her analogy. No one had ever accused him of fitting into polite society.

His bread and butter as an undercover cop had been to blend in with the worst possible segment of society. But Lexi saw something better in him, something semi-noble.

"I can't have what I want, either, Josh, but assuming you didn't come here to tell me you changed your mind and want to claim me as your own, I'm just going to head on back to the party before I'm missed.''

He cuffed her wrist with his fingers, the gesture bringing back out-of-control memories about last weekend's handcuff adventures. ''I have questions to ask you first.''

She waited, her body resting very still, only a fraction of an inch away from his. Her perfume teased his nose, fired his senses. He wanted to touch her, taste her, keep her captive, with his hands as her only bonds this time.

Then again, maybe he really wished he didn't have to hold her to make her stay.

''QUESTIONS?'' Lexi's brain was fuzzy—make that sexually scrambled—by Josh's presence. She forced herself to remember this kind of interlude was all Josh wanted from her—private, anonymous, physical.

He didn't want to take on all of her. For that matter, he didn't even know all of her. He still saw her as the wild child, the bad girl who knew how to cause a scene and stir up trouble.

She stepped away from him, right into a wall of coats, to prevent herself from getting sucked in by sheer animal magnetism. ''What questions?''

Josh let go of her wrist, his jaw working overtime as he clenched his teeth in obvious sexual frustration that mirrored her own. ''My case against the Bertrands is nonexistent.''

Her mind struggled to shake off the steam they generated just by standing next to one another. ''I called your office last week and told them Simone definitely purchased one of Valentino's red cashmere sweaters. Didn't you get my message?''

"The lab is still testing the fibers."

Indignation fired her steps in his direction, until she stood toe to toe with the man. He hadn't once bothered to comment on her new haircut—but he could question her knowledge of fabric? ''You think I don't know cashmere from acrylic?''

He might have responded, but Lexi cut him off.

"I didn't get to be where I am today by not knowing every flipping thing there is to know about clothes, Josh. You may think my job is some sort of superficial B.S., but it entertains a lot of people, and I gain a lot of social leverage for other causes through what I do." Call her defensive, but hadn't Amanda promised that people saw beyond the outward trappings of Lexi's glamorous lifestyle?

"I know."

"It's not global economics, maybe, but it's— You do?" Had she heard him correctly? She backed up a step in an already confined space.

He followed, stalking her. "I know your work is important." He fingered one shoulder-length curl of her hair. "You accomplish big things by wielding a mighty pen and providing a living example of unselfishness. You don't ever need to defend yourself to me."

No man had ever spoken such sweet words to her. Certainly her family never had. She considered throwing herself in his arms and taking whatever relationship he could offer her, but he swiftly changed the subject.

"I trust your gut about the fibers, Lexi, but until I get more scientific proof that Simone has a sweater made of that fabric, I can't get a warrant to search her place, and I don't have much to go on." He let go of the curl he'd been holding so that it sprang back into place beside her cheek. "I need something more concrete."

Although Lexi still felt the warmth of Josh's professed admiration, his conversation reminded her that he wasn't here to sneak a quickie in the cloakroom or to boost her ego. He was a committed police detective, a man dedicated to protecting hapless fashion critics and anyone else who might find themselves the target of criminal activity.

She admired his work, too, respected him for his noble ideals. But that didn't help close the gap between them.

"And you think you might somehow find the evidence you need tonight?" Lexi eased away from him, staring at the wall of coats to distract herself from the too tempting detective. "Simone is here, if she's still a suspect."

"She and her brother are both suspects, along with several other guests tonight."

That snagged her attention. "You think Anton is behind some of this?" She found it hard to reconcile her playground savior with an arsonist.

He went utterly still. "You have reason to think he wouldn't be?"

The sudden chill in the room made Lexi long to wrap herself in one of the warm shawls tossed across a back counter. Although even cashmere made a poor substitute for Josh's arms.

"Only that I thought we were friends. But I guess it makes sense he wouldn't want me to pan Simone's designs in my column if he is the driving force behind her business." She thought through the verbiage of the anonymous letters, the vague pleas for her to quit running her mouth. "The letter writer obviously wants me to shut up about something, but I've never been able to pinpoint exactly what."

Josh tensed, leaned forward. "But you have criticized Simone's designs on more than one occasion?"

"I prefer 'critique' to 'criticize,' but yes, I've nixed several of Simone's designs in my column."

"I see." Josh nodded, his gaze remote, the wheels in his detective mind visibly spinning.

She waved a hand in front of his face. "Does that mean, 'I see, Anton is guilty as sin' or 'I see, Simone has been behind this all along'?"

Josh caught her hand in midair and held it captive in front of his face. Lexi startled at the sudden shift in his mood. His gaze cleared, focused solely on her.

"It means, I see I have more work to do." He brought the heel of her hand closer to his mouth. "I see I can't think straight around you." He bent her finger back ever so slightly and ran his tongue around the hollow of her arched palm. "And I see I don't stand a chance in hell of not touching you once I get within fifteen—maybe twenty-five—feet of you."

The warm swirl of his tongue made her knees weak, her thighs shivery. He kept his eyes on her, cataloging her reactions, silently challenging her to deny the heat between them.

She wouldn't. Couldn't.

Josh's mouth in silence was more eloquent than hers at full speed. And *Gawd* was the man speaking volumes to her right now.

She allowed her eyes to drift closed, telling herself she only wanted a moment to concentrate on the sensation of his lips sliding over her flesh. But closing her eyes made her less cautious, less able to remember why she couldn't give herself completely to this man. In that narrow window of time, Josh managed to draw her body to his, stroke the bare skin of her back with his fingers, tease the edges of her gown with his touch.

Josh heard the hitch in Lexi's breathing, sensed a hunger in her that equaled his own. He toyed with the sequined edge of her dress, so low on her back, so dangerously seductive.

If he slipped his palm beneath the fabric, would he find the lure of leopard-print panties? Or, considering the way her gown molded to her like a second skin, would he find her naked and waiting for him?

A cloakroom wasn't the place to find out, especially not with New York's fashion elite gathered in force just outside the flimsy shade pulled down over the front counter. He told himself he would stop any minute, but then Lexi's hand reached to cover his, squeeze his, nudge his fingers lower....

The groan that escaped him was lost in the driving bass rhythm of the dance tune pounding through the club. He dipped into the curve of her back, his knuckles brushing the thin material that held the sequin network in place.

Her skin taunted him, vibrant and warm as if she'd spent the day lying in the sun. He curved a hand over her bottom, all the while searching for the slightest scrap of satin or silk, yet finding her deliciously naked.

The knowledge that she wore absolutely nothing beneath her gown drove him insane. He crushed her to him, needing to feel the gentle shape of her breasts against his chest. He squeezed her hip and reached lower still, needing to feel—

"Josh, wait."

Through the sex-starved recesses of his overwhelmed senses, Josh heard Lexi's soft plea.

He stilled his hands, but kept her in his arms, powerless to let her go just yet. "What?"

Her breath blew along his shoulder in one long, frustrated sigh. "We can't do this."

He tried blinking his way back to reality. The senses that had been focused solely on her slowly registered the outside world once again. "Wrong place. I know."

She shook her head against him. "Wrong everything, remember?"

Damn. "Not the wrong chemistry, Lex. Admit that much." He forced his arms to his side, his body protesting the loss of her.

"I admit that much." Smoothing her gown over her hips, she stretched her lips into a wistful smile. "For all the good it does."

More curses came to his mind. He knew he wasn't

supposed to touch her anymore, knew she wasn't the kind of woman for half measures. Yet here he was, trying to take whatever he could in a damn coat closet.

"I'm sorry—"

She covered his lips with manicured fingers, the pink nail polish glittering with those tiny silver fish. "Don't be."

She oozed sophistication and glamour, but there was nothing refined or tame about her. Lexi's gown was wild and daring, baring scandalous amounts of skin while still maintaining her classy edge.

"You look gorgeous tonight," he whispered across the super-charged three inches of air between them.

"Thank you."

"I like your hair." He plucked a springy curl from her shoulder and smoothed the strand between his fingers. "You must have cut off about two feet."

"Twenty-six inches."

He remembered her hair blanketing him in her bed and missed the rest of it for just a moment. No, he mostly just missed her in his bed. "You measured it?"

A smile kicked up one corner of her mouth. "It's standard procedure to measure it when you donate it. I cut it off for one of those places that make wigs for kids who've undergone chemo or who've lost their hair for some other reason."

Her words provided a knockout punch to his ego. He'd told himself he was making a difference in the city by taking bad guys off the street, but he'd ended up nearly costing a fellow cop's life by giving a ju-venile gangster a second chance.

Yet Lexi continually managed to give help where it was needed—finding research money for kids with incurable illnesses, lending her name to the Shelter the Homeless fund-raiser despite the gossip she'd faced that night, and lifting an anonymous child's spirits by cutting off her gorgeous hair. Josh won-dered if he'd be as likely to make an impact on the city by joining Lexi in her crusade to better the world as he did roaming the streets anonymously with a gun and a badge.

But he wasn't about to share that thought with her. He'd worked his whole adult life as a cop. He wasn't ready to be relegated to the role of Lexi's personal bodyguard, no matter how enticing her body might be.

"For a woman who likes to dress in sequins and glitter, you've got to be the least superficial person I've ever met." He replaced the lone curl back in the shiny mass of her hair.

She edged toward the door. "I'd better get back out there.

Josh realized he'd blown his professional objective of finding out more about the Bertrands when he'd opted to kiss Lexi instead of talk to her. Before he could ask her to stay a little longer, however, the thin shade over the front counter opened.

"Anyone in here?" An impatient feminine voice pierced the air.

Josh turned to see Ms. WonderLift herself at the cloakroom desk, a gray fur draped over one arm.

Dressed head to toe in white satin and diamonds, she didn't look much like an arsonist, but Josh wasn't taking any chances.

"Hello, Simone." Lexi held out her sparkly nails to take the coat. "Please say this is fake. This is a cloakroom, not a kennel, you know."

"Would I dare risk your delicate sensibilities by showing up here with a dead animal on my shoulder?" She lit a cigarette while waiting for Lexi to bring her a numbered tag for the wrap. "You've shot me down in your column enough times this month, I think."

Lexi stuffed the fur on a back table and handed Simone a tag. Josh doubted Lexi had any clue how the cloakroom system actually worked, but then again, she probably didn't give a rip whether or not Simone ever retrieved her coat.

"Yet you didn't bother to put in an appearance at the homeless benefit last week to revel in the glory of your letter to my editor." Lexi picked up a guest book on the cloakroom counter and fanned away the smoke from Simone's cigarette. "So unlike you not to gloat."

Simone shrugged, allowing one thin strap of her dress to slip off her shoulder. "That was James's fault. He knew I wanted to go, so he gave the chauffeur the night off, then he pretended not to know the phone numbers for any driver services. I could have killed him."

"Get out." Lexi slammed the guest book on the counter. "He didn't tell me that."

Josh couldn't help but think their conversation

sounded reasonably friendly, as archrivals went. He hadn't expected Simone to be so up-front with Lexi. In fact, something about Simone's slouchy body language, her hangdog expression, made him think the woman admired and envied Lexi more than she hated her.

"Of course he wouldn't. James is much too refined to brag when he gets the best of me." Simone smoothed her hair back from her face and fluffed the curls around her neck. "Next time I take a potshot, you can bet I'll remember to plan the follow-up in advance."

Lexi rolled her eyes. "Does your life have to be a continual plot against me? You are like Cruella De Vil. Or maybe one of the villains from Scooby Doo, Simone. If you spent more time on your designs and less on how to piss me off, you'd probably come up with something marginally successful."

Simone raised a perfectly plucked eyebrow. "You think so, do you?"

"Your taste isn't that bad." Lexi pointed in the direction of Simone's dress. "I mean, this is cute, and it's obviously original."

Josh would bet the bank that the pleasure in Simone's eyes was genuine. He'd made a career in the shadows, reading people as Duke talked to them, interpreting gestures and tone of voice. He knew how to discern people's secrets and emotions.

The fledgling designer practically hung over the cloakroom counter to confide in Lexi. "Some of the best things seem to come to me in a flash. I had a vision for this dress and then *kaboom*—I practically just cut it out of the satin like this." Simone paused a moment, as if remembering herself and the hauteur she normally exuded. "I mean, when you are ready to retract all those mean things you've said about my previous designs, I'd be happy to show you a few of my new things."

With one final puff of cigarette, Simone turned and sauntered off into the crowd.

"You see what I put up with?" Lexi demanded, fanning the stale air in the cloakroom with her hand. "She's always been that way."

"She wants your approval." Josh mentally moved Simone lower on his list of suspects. He didn't care what Lexi said about the cashmere sweater fibers; Simone's attitude didn't strike him as that of a woman out to kill—or even necessarily scare—Lexi.

"She wants my head on a platter, you mean. Didn't we agree she might be the one responsible for nearly barbecuing Muffin last week?"

"I'm changing my mind." Josh didn't have time to sort through the whole knot right now, because the complexion of his case was changing. He needed to find out what Anton Bertrand was doing tonight, and then he needed to scout informants for the scoop on a potential shipment to the city this weekend. "I've got some work to do tonight, but I might need your help tomorrow."

"I don't know, Josh. I thought I was helping you when you called me in here to ask me questions, but I ended up nearly hiking up a two-thousand-dollar dress in a coatroom of all places."

Josh barely leashed his hands to his side at her

mention of hiking up that damn dress. He wanted a second chance with her so badly it hurt.

And it would keep on hurting if he kept recalling how nothing separated her naked body from him but a frail web of sequins.

Focus. On. Work.

"Tomorrow is for real, Lex. If Anton is really our man, I have an idea how we might ferret him out. But I can't do it without your help."

She walked her fingers up his tie and tapped his chin with one painted talon. "You're beginning to see you can't operate without me, aren't you."

No kidding. The woman was like a time bomb dropped into his world, and he was fool enough to keep coming back for more.

Her touch robbed him of thought. "You are pretty damn addictive, Lex."

She hovered beside him for one more moment, her gaze locked on his. Then, perhaps satisfied with his answer, she slipped away again. Turning to open the door to the club, Lexi practically ran into her missing-in-action bodyguard, Otis.

Josh made a note to read the guy the riot act before he left Lexi in his care again.

Lexi smiled at Otis and then tossed a simmering look over her shoulder at Josh. "You think I'm addictive now, wait 'til you hit next week and you start going through the withdrawal symptoms on your own." She smiled that sinful, knowing smile that drove him wild. "You're going to be toast, hot stuff."

Josh watched her walk away, a seductive shimmy in her hips she'd no doubt put there for his benefit.

He was about ready to rip an overcoat off the wall to hide the evidence of his addiction, but instead, he settled for remaining behind a table full of coats for a minute.

He'd be toast next week?

Hell, he was already sizzling his way into a slow burn right now.

14

TWELVE HOURS after she'd sashayed away from Josh
Winger, Lexi stood in the middle of assorted rolling
racks at Amanda's loft, agonizing over what to wear
the next time she saw him. Why couldn't she content
herself with the great exit line she'd come up with
yesterday? Did she have to throw herself back in his
path again now?

Of course she did. He had finally admitted he
wanted her to help him out on his big drug smuggling
case, and she wouldn't let him down. By dismissing
their personal relationship in favor of his professional
life, Josh had about torn her heart out, but she refused
to allow her hurt to show. No one but Muffin ever
saw her cry.

Right now, she simply needed to focus on wardrobe and get her mind off the twinge she felt at the
thought of seeing him one last time. Resolutely, she
stared at the tartan plaid miniskirt and the red cat suit,
trying to decide which to wear for her first foray into
police work. Deciding she'd rather go with a nod to
Sherlock Holmes than an ode to the *Mod Squad*, Lexi
pulled out the tiny plaid miniskirt and an oversize
cream-colored blazer.

Josh might not need her for anything but investigative help, but by God, she was going to deliver the most inspired crime-busting effort she possibly could. And she might as well make a lasting impression, because after today, she couldn't imagine she'd ever see him again.

"His loss, right, Muffin?" Damn the tear itching behind her eyes.

The poodle barked her approval, but Snowball remained silent in her place on a nearby throw rug, her pink bow drooping into one eye. Lexi knew exactly how she felt.

Sighing, she wriggled her way into her skirt. She needed to have caught a cab out to Long Island five minutes ago, but she hated to leave with Snowball so pitiful.

"Girls, we don't need any man in our lives who can't give all of himself." Lexi brushed out her curls and clipped a rhinestone barrette into her shorter hair. Losing two feet of black curls paled in comparison to losing the most intriguing—warmest—man she'd ever met. "If Josh Winger would rather be Joe Super Stealth Detective than our man, then we don't want him, anyway, okay?"

Snowball made a little whine, then settled her doggy chin on her front paws with a sigh.

"I'll have none of that." Lexi shook her hairbrush for emphasis, questioning who she was really trying to convince. "We didn't work our way into New York's limelight by skulking around with a guy who doesn't want to claim us in public."

Although Lexi had to admit, she found herself wondering if she might be ready to take an occasional reprieve from the intense glare of the media spotlight. Her time with Josh had made her realize she wanted more time for herself now and then. Between her job and her causes, her life held little else.

Someday, it might be nice to have time to hang out at home with a decent guy. Bake some cookies. Watch a few more episodes of *The View*. Josh helped her appreciate how far she'd come from the woman with such low self-esteem that she took self-defense classes to lift herself up.

Now Lexi was at the top of her game, succeeding on every professional level of her life—but did it matter when she didn't have anyone to share it with? She was definitely ready for more than an occasional one-night stand. She was ready for a real relationship.

She just couldn't imagine wanting that relationship with anyone other than Josh.

Grabbing Amanda's favorite trench coat from the hall closet, Lexi blew kisses to her dogs and tried to convince herself she wasn't giving up the man of her dreams. She was just growing up, growing into who she really wanted to be.

The fact that it hurt like hell, that she'd rather be home sighing listlessly with Snowball than facing the man responsible for breaking her heart, was just an unhappy coincidence.

But she was Lexi Mansfield, internationally known fashion critic, for crying out loud. She wouldn't go down with a whimper and a sigh. And if Josh Winger thought she would just fade quietly into the background, he had another thing coming.

Today she intended to show him exactly what he

was giving up by letting her go. And—petty or not—she couldn't wait to watch him eat his heart out.

JOSH STARED OUT the front windshield of the surveillance van he and Duke had signed out for their sting operation today. A light rain blurred his view, dulling everything in the fast-food restaurant parking lot to cloudy gray.

"I still don't understand why we didn't just pick her up in the city," Duke grumbled from the back of the van, where he helped a technician check the sound equipment.

"Otis is going to intercept her before she takes a cab. They should be here any minute." Josh glanced at his watch for the tenth time in the past three minutes.

Duke yanked aside the curtain separating the front and back of the van to glare at Josh. "What I'm asking is why the hell don't you care enough about her to be on her doorstep this morning, Columbo. For a guy that had his hand up her skirt last weekend, you're really pissing me off with how you're treating Amanda's best friend."

"She cut me loose, man." She might as well have cut off his whole damn arm for how off balance she'd thrown him. But Josh couldn't afford to think about that today—not when his case was riding on Lexi's cooperation. "There's not much I can do about that."

"You can fight for her, moron." Duke thumped Josh's head with two fingers. "I've seen you take down escaped convicts and crack-head psychos with nothing but your bare hands, yet you can't tell a five-foot china doll you care about her?''

"China? Try Teflon. She's as tough as they come." Tough enough to take on enemies bigger than a crack-head psycho. Lexi Mansfield would probably end drug abuse in New York by sheer force of will.

Josh checked his watch again, wondering if he should have escorted Lexi to the meeting site himself. He'd been avoiding unnecessary exposure to temptation when he asked Otis to drive her to Long Island, but Josh would never forgive himself if his lack of willpower where she was concerned ended up getting her hurt.

Just as Josh picked up his cell phone to call Otis for a status report, Stanton's unmarked police car pulled into the drive-thru lane. Taking calming breaths, Josh tried to wipe away the condensation on the van windshield to get a better picture of the woman seated next to the rookie cop, but she remained a gray blur.

She was clear enough in his mind, however. Lexi had branded herself onto Josh's consciousness with one click of her handcuffs.

Josh eased out of his seat and reached for the door. "She deserves a hell of a lot better than me, anyway."

"She deserves a guy who will fight for her, that's for damn sure." Duke stared at his friend critically. "But you're not that bad. A little rough around the edges, maybe, but probably workable from a female perspective."

"Thanks for that glowing assessment." Josh

pushed open the van door, ready to do whatever he could to close his eyes to the lure of Lexi.

Duke joined him in the sliding doorway of the van, and the two of them stared out into the misty rain toward Otis's car. A long, lean leg appeared out of the passenger side door before being joined by a second gorgeous gam.

Lexi Mansfield eased out of the car, clad in a trench coat that flapped open in the breeze—and underneath it was the tiniest miniskirt Josh had ever seen. She turned heads all over the parking lot with her I-mean-business strut and her I-mean-pleasure legs.

Josh groaned. How the hell had he ever convinced himself he could ignore this woman's appeal?

Duke whistled under his breath for about half a second before Josh nailed him in the gut with his elbow.

He waved Lexi over to the van and said to Duke between clenched teeth, "Be-freaking-have."

Duke rubbed an absent hand over his wounded solar plexus. "She's a pistol, Columbo."

Josh glared his partner into silence, as Lexi neared the van and held her hand out to be helped inside.

Shiny red nails, no flashing fish today.

Duke reached for her first, totally irritating Josh. Josh nudged him out of the way with one shoulder and took Lexi's hand.

"Hello, Winger." Her voice slid over him like she slid her fingers inside his palm. Was it his imagination, or did she stroke the center of his hand with one finger? She let go as soon as she got both feet inside the vehicle, her dark gaze roving over the high-tech surveillance equipment instead of him.

Josh nodded toward a vacant seat amid the gadgetry. "Have a seat."

Straightening his tie, he tried to rein in his runaway thoughts and keep his eyes off her legs as she eased around him. Exotic perfume teased his nose, enticing him to sniff out its source and take a taste.

She slipped into the swiveling captain's chair in the back, while Duke—thankfully—made himself scarce in the driver's seat up front on the other side of the curtain.

Without looking out the window, Josh knew Duke was pulling out of the fast-food parking lot and following Stanton's car toward the Bertrands' neighborhood.

Lexi crossed her legs with boarding school grace, a feat he wouldn't have thought possible in that short skirt. Her dangling foot twitched and flexed a mere two inches away from him.

"So what gives, tiger?" She stared him down with unblinking brown eyes. "Are you roping me into your cloak-and-dagger world today?"

"Only for an hour or so." He left it unsaid that they'd have no reason to run into one another again. No excuses for one- or two-night stands. With Lexi's help, Josh could secure a warrant for Anton's house and either cross him off his list or nail him for taking part in the smuggling operation that had gone down last night, according to the precinct's informants. "And only if you feel comfortable doing what I'm going to ask of you."

"Shoot." She fidgeted in her seat and re-crossed her legs.

Her nylon-clad calf brushed his leg, causing immediate shockwaves through his veins and sending a message of animal hunger to his brain. Didn't she have any idea what her restless energy did to him?

She smiled innocently and waited.

He shifted in his seat. Cleared his throat. Focused on the fact that Anton Bertrand could be connected to the biggest smuggling system in the city. Bertrand could also be connected to the rampant recruitment of minors for the dirty work.

A fact that nudged some semblance of coherent thought into his sex-fogged brain. "I need you to talk to Simone and her brother today. One of them, both of them, whoever will say more to you."

"Lucky you, talking is one of my strong suits." Her voice was throaty and deep, as if she hadn't had reason to use it much since she'd crawled out of bed this morning.

Thinking about Lexi and bed at the same time could only lead to trouble. He fished around some scattered notes on the floor beside him and seized a map of the Bertrands' house. Anything to keep his hands busy and off the temptation sitting two inches in front of him.

"We'll be out here in the van." He pointed to a spot across the street. "And we'll be listening to your conversation, assuming you don't mind going in there with a tiny microphone taped inside your...um..." His gaze roved over her outfit—the tiny skirt, the scant silk blouse, the blazer that was nearly as long as the skirt. "...jacket."

Not waiting for any further instruction, she wriggled her way out of the only substantial piece of clothing she wore. Bare arms emerged from the long blazer. Her shoulders were covered with nothing but the tiny straps of her blouse. A blouse that dipped low enough to hint at the gentle swell of her breasts.

"I'm ready." She held her arms out at her sides, offering herself—her body—to him.

Had he really talked himself into being noble? Had he honestly thought that even if he walked away from his career field, he shouldn't be with her because she deserved somebody highbrow and sophisticated, someone who moved in the same world she did?

Because right about now, with her teasing eyes glancing up and down his body, all that noble thinking sounded like bullshit to him. Thank God, Duke had drawn the curtain between the driver's seat and the cargo area.

Josh threw the map onto the narrow counter full of computer equipment and tugged her hands back down into her lap. He leaned forward into her personal space, nose to nose with her. "Do you have any idea what you are doing?"

The question worked on several levels, and right now, he didn't really care which version she answered.

Something dark and maybe even a little dangerous glittered in her eyes. "Offering up my services, Josh. Isn't that what you wanted?"

His sexually skewed vision cleared for just a moment—long enough to take in the defiant tilt of her chin, the purposeful pout of her lips. "You're playing me like a damn harp today, aren't you."

Her breathing was quick, shallow. Josh watched her chest rise and fall with each little pant.

"Only if you're going to try and pretend you don't want me."

He released her wrists before he had a chance to do something stupid…like draw her to the van floor and relive their wrestling match. "It's not that I'm pretending, Lexi. I'm just playing by your rules—all or nothing, right?"

"Oh, please. I said 'all or nothing,' and yet I'm settling for a pretty damn painful gray area by making out with you in a cloakroom or by running to your side today to help you out. You can at least do me the courtesy of acting like you know I exist and that we've shared more than a cup of coffee together. You got it?"

Hell, yes, he got it. In his quest to be noble, he'd forgotten a basic rule of play when it came to this woman. *Lexi hates to be ignored.*

He brushed a hand along the side of her cheek, allowing his fingertips to graze her smooth skin, his knuckles to dip into the dark curls framing her face.

Her eyelashes fluttered for a split second, tempting him to give her more attention than she was ready to handle right now—but this wasn't the time. Nor was it the place. Besides, no matter what she said about hating to be ignored, Josh knew she wouldn't settle for anything but everything from him.

She opened her eyes and pinned him with her gaze

as they rolled closer to Simone's Long Island mansion. "So who's going to put their hands down my blouse to attach the microphone? You or me?"

IN THE LOGICAL RECESSES of her mind, Lexi thought she should probably be at least a little scared as she walked up the steps to Simone's for her first undercover operation. But frustration fueled her steps as she trekked across the brick walkway, her breath fanning out in white puffs through the cool fall air.

Despite her best effort at sensual enticement, Josh had made her do her own microphone installation, staunchly refusing to put his hands anywhere near her bare skin. Damn the man.

His reluctance would have made the Lexi of a month ago believe she had all the allure of a houseplant. Not anymore. If nothing else, her relationship with Josh had given her a confidence in herself she'd searched for through self-defense classes, outrageous clothes and outspoken opinions.

Although those things had bolstered her after a lifetime of being ignored by her busy parents, they hadn't come close to assuaging her pride the way Josh's hungry gaze had.

Too bad he wasn't willing to act on that hunger anymore. He'd turned his back in the van when she'd executed the perfect shimmy out of her silk blouse, all the while barking out instructions for what to ask Simone during their discussion this afternoon. She was thankful that Duke had remained safely on the other side of the curtain during their discussion. By now, however, Josh's partner would be with him in the back of the van, listening to her wire transmission.

Lexi pressed the doorbell and waited impatiently for James to answer the summons. She would ask all the right questions, elicit the answers Josh needed and then retreat to her own corner after this round. Josh might be willing to risk his neck for her fish or her parakeet, but he didn't seem to want to put his heart on the line for *her*.

The leaded glass front door swung open. "Good afternoon, Alexandra," James greeted her, his butler delivery as flawless as ever. "You're looking lovely today."

Lexi edged past him into the foyer, hoping for James's sake that the Bertrands weren't involved in anything illegal. She twirled on her heel, however, forcing herself to act the same as usual. "I'm wearing vintage Marc Jacobs, Jeeves. What else do you expect?"

"Vintage Marc Jacobs? In my day, my dear, we called that wearing a lot of leg." The sly old devil winked at her, although his precise elocution never wavered. "Shall I see if the lady of the house is home?"

"Simone and Anton both, please," Lexi requested, idly wondering what Josh and Duke thought of her performance so far. She knew they were listening outside in the surveillance vehicle; they'd triple-checked her tiny sound system before she'd entered the house.

James skipped the bow he normally made to more formal guests, but he still added a butler-ish "If you would care for a seat in the parlor?'' before he disappeared upstairs.

He left Lexi to make her way into the front room and to wonder if Josh was already plotting his return to his quiet, anonymous life. With a quiet, easy-to-manage woman. Lexi had no idea what sort of woman he normally dated, but she had the feeling she herself was the anomaly.

"I bet your usual one-night stand wouldn't put herself on the line for your damn job,'' she muttered to herself and any stubborn men listening to her via the microphone. She wandered into the parlor to wait.

The room was mercifully devoid of silver statues, decorated French country style with everything in shades of cream and white. Gold picture frames and gold tassels on the white throw pillows grounded the room. As with Simone's clothing designs, her mishmash of decorating schemes proved she had a great eye for design—she just didn't always know how to use it.

Simone glided into the room first, wearing a burgundy satin smoking jacket Lexi would have killed for. Of course, Simone was actually smoking in it, so she trailed a cloud in her wake and tickled Lexi's nose with fumes.

"Gawd, Simone, how does James put up with you and your vices?'' Lexi fanned the air with an architecture magazine she'd picked up from the sofa table.

Simone flung herself onto the sofa and propped her feet on a matching white ottoman. "He usually ices me into compliance by blasting the air conditioner, but I think he feels sorry for me today because I have a hangover.'' She took one last long drag on the cigarette, then stubbed it out in a crystal bowl that had no business being used as an ashtray. ''So to what do I owe the pleasure? Have you decided to retract all your nasty statements about my designs?''

Lexi tried to see past the woman's biting tone, wondering if there could be anything to Josh's insistence that Simone secretly envied her.

Hard to believe, judging by the designer's smug expression.

''Not exactly.'' Lexi stalled, revamping her approach to this discussion in light of the fact that Anton hadn't entered the parlor yet. Josh was most interested in confirming that Anton ran Simone's business—a fact that apparently wasn't supported in any legal or tax documents. ''After our chat last night, I thought I'd come by and see some of your new designs. Is the jacket yours?''

Lexi plunked down on the couch beside her and fingered the silk of the smoking jacket.

''You like it?'' Simone looked stunned, as if she'd swallowed a horse.

''I love it.'' Which was the honest truth, but Lexi still felt guilty for engaging in this conversation when she had ulterior motives of information gathering.

Simone jumped off the couch as if her hangover was a long-forgotten memory. Pulling a thick sketch pad out of the bookcase lining one white wall, she kept up a running monologue. ''I've got a ton of new stuff in here, but I'm only producing about half this fall. I never thought you'd really give me a fair shake,

Lex. I mean, you've always been so bitchy to me—
no offense.''

Lexi fought the urge to quibble about who had been
bitchy all these years. After all, *Lexi* hadn't been the
one cutting off the hair on all of Simone's Barbie
dolls or stealing Simone's homework assignments for
French class.

Instead, as Simone shoved her design book in
Lexi's lap, she seized on a piece of information she
thought Josh might be able to use. ''You're only producing half of these?''

Anton chose that moment to join them, clearing his
throat in the doorway. ''Well, if this isn't an unusual
sight. I never thought I would see Snow White and
the Wicked Queen sitting down over a sketch pad
together.''

He wore a taupe suit that might have been Hugo
Boss, but it had seen better days. In fact, his whole
ensemble looked like he'd slept in it. A teenage boy
trailed in Anton's wake wearing beat-up jeans and a
jacket with high-tech designer sneakers that might
have been just lifted out of the box.

''Hi, Anton.'' Lexi smiled at Simone's brother.
''Who's your friend?''

Anton pulled on his shirt cuffs and straightened his
tie. ''This is Brad. We're going to play tennis.''

The boy didn't look like Anton's usual tennis partners, but that was hardly her business. Before she
could give it any more thought, Simone nudged her
and pointed to a purple smoking jacket on the first
page of her book.

The design on paper was more contrived than the

slouch version Simone wore, but Lexi was too aware of her mission now to concentrate on the designs. "It's gorgeous, Simone, but why aren't you producing all these?"

"Because Anton is very stingy," Simone supplied, flipping forward a few pages in the book. "He said there was no point in making them all, since you would pan them, anyway. Apparently, we lose money whenever you gripe about my clothes in your column."

As much as it grated, Lexi decided to play stupid for purposes of the surveillance tape. "We? I thought Simone Bertrand Designs was your company, Simone."

Simone frowned.

Anton lit a cigarette from the pack Simone had left lying on the sofa table. An intriguing move on his part, considering Lexi had never seen him smoke.

"It is Simone's company, Lex," he answered smoothly. "But as her brother, I try to give her advice on how to conduct the business soundly."

"Oh, please." Simone snorted. "You mean, you choose which checks to write for me. I could have had a good year in the magazines if Lexi liked my things and said so in her column, Anton. You should have let me trust my instincts and produce all the designs."

Anton strode over to Lexi and slammed the book shut in her lap. Lexi noticed the boy—Brad—jumped at the sound.

"We wouldn't have had enough money to finance

them all, anyway, Simone.'' He smiled as he said it, but the words were edged with anger, frustration.

Or was Lexi just being paranoid?

Either way, her work here seemed to be done. She'd wrested an admission that Anton was writing the checks for Simone's business. Maybe now Josh could get his warrant to follow up on the arson and smuggling investigations.

Lexi set the design book aside and rose from the couch. ''We can always talk about this over lunch next week, Simone. Or else just make sure to invite me to your show—''

''No!'' Simone grabbed Lexi by the arm. ''Now is a fine time.'' She reached for her sketches, glaring at her brother. ''Anton and Brad are on their way to play tennis anyway, right?''

Anton paced and smoked, not answering for a moment.

Lexi held her breath, hoping like hell he would just leave.

Finally, he nodded.

Lexi sighed in relief as quietly as she could.

But after he ground out his cigarette in the crystal dish, he headed right toward her.

Once again, Lexi tensed.

Anton stopped a few inches in front of her and held his cheek out for her to kiss.

The age-old hello and goodbye gesture of the design world suddenly turned her stomach. Still, if it signaled the man's exit...

Lexi had leaned forward to kiss the air beside his

jaw when he grabbed with both hands and turned his lips to hers to kiss her full on the mouth.

In the back of her mind, she registered Simone's squeal of disgust at Anton's breach of etiquette as Lexi pushed at Anton's shoulders. Too late, she realized she should have protected her body instead of shoving at his. He groped her right through her silk shell until his hand landed on—

"A wire." He broke off the kiss and ripped the small microphone from its nestling place between her breasts.

She stared at the little piece of electronic equipment for one horrified moment. Lexi wobbled as she spun on her heel to run, cursing Manolo Blahniks for the first time in her life.

"Not so fast." Anton grabbed her before she could go anywhere, producing a sleek black gun from his waistband. He pulled Lexi back to his chest, tucking the gun up under her rib cage for good measure. "I've been safeguarding your scrawny butt from Simone since you were ten. You can damn well pay me back with a little protection today, Alexandra."

15

JOSH EXPLODED through the van door as soon as the tap went dead. He charged across the lawn into the bushes just below the Bertrands' parlor window.

He cursed Anton Bertrand, but not nearly as much as he cursed himself for putting Lexi in danger.

How the hell had a simple dig for information escalated into a hostage situation in the course of five seconds? From the muffled sounds on the other end of the surveillance tape, Josh hadn't been able to tell what had happened in the few moments Anton was supposedly saying his goodbyes. But after hearing Simone's cry, Lexi's muffled yell and the recording turn to static, Josh hadn't waited around to discuss the implications of the sounds.

Lexi was in trouble. Big, no-holds-barred, damn trouble. All because of Josh's impatience with his drug case and his stupid-ass decision to capitalize on Lexi's relationship with the Bertrands to gather more information.

As the sound of static had filled the van, Josh had burst out of the vehicle to sprint across the lawn, Duke on his heels. Duke had taken one side of the house, and Josh had taken the other; presumably, Otis would be calling for backup.

Now Josh eased himself up to the windowsill and peered inside, grateful he'd studied the floor plan of the home.

He was just in time to see Anton Bertrand hustle his sister and Lexi out of the room through a narrow archway in the back, while some kid Josh didn't recognize locked the front door to the parlor behind them.

The teen's patched jeans and threadbare shirt paired with two-hundred-dollar sneakers reminded Josh of another kid he'd tangled with in the course of his drug case. A juvenile offender who hadn't blinked at shooting a cop—and who'd wound up dead.

Josh willed the kid to hurry, because as soon as Gangster Junior was out of the room, Josh would be through the window to follow Lexi.

Seconds dragged on in slow motion until the teen's sneakers sped off under the archway. Josh poised his gun, ready to punch his way through the glass—until the locked parlor door opened from the hallway. He cursed the delay, wondering who the hell else could be in the house for him to have to take on....

Jeeves.

Josh banged on the window as the Bertrand butler was reaching for the telephone. He trusted Lexi's instincts that the man wouldn't be involved in the family's shady dealings.

Besides, he needed all the help he could get.

James moved across the parlor like a rookie showing off his most impressive moves. The old guy pried the window open and shoved a floor lamp out of Josh's way.

"I was just about to call the police. He's got Alexandra—"

Josh hauled himself into the house and pushed past the butler. "Where?" He was already headed toward the archway in the back of the room.

James shadowed him, keeping pace step for step. "My guess is the wine cellar. Two rights and a left, then down the stairs."

"Got it." Josh started running before the words left his mouth. "Let my partner in," he shouted over his shoulder. "And then you'd better make tracks out of the house."

Even from three rooms away, he could hear the old man's answer, "Like hell."

Shit. The last thing Josh needed was for another civilian to get mixed up in his hostage situation, although he had to admire a man who looked out for Lexi. Hell, the old-timer could probably take care of her better than Josh did. Surely Mr. Manners never would have allowed Lexi to involve herself in a high-stakes smuggling case.

Two rights and a left later, Josh tore down the stairs to an arched wooden door with a sophisticated locking mechanism. He stared at the computerized keypad, wondering if he should risk wasting more time with an effort to jam the code and open the lock, or if he should follow his impatient trigger finger and simply start shooting at the security device.

Frustration coiled inside him along with a healthy dose of fear. Fear for Lexi. Fear that he wouldn't play something out right and she'd wind up getting hurt because of him.

Still, logic won out. Josh ran a series of quick tests on the keypad and succeeded in jamming the mechanism. He slipped inside the door without a sound, but from the depths of the darkened cellar, Anton's voice halted him.

"Every step you take puts the glamour queen a little more at risk, Winger."

Josh couldn't see three feet in front of him in the shadowed cellar, but he could hear a woman crying. The sound wrenched his gut, reminding him how selfish he'd been to involve Lexi in this mess.

God knows, he would not risk his glamour queen by moving another inch. Lexi in danger made this worse than the worst moment he'd ever had on the job. For her, he'd have to bide his time. Wait until his eyes adjusted and he could see what the hell he was doing.

"I'm not going anywhere." Josh raised his arms, gun still in his hand.

"Throw down your weapons where I can see them."

Josh traced the voice to the far corner of the room as he tossed aside his gun. Squinting into the shadows, he spied the outline of a man in a light-colored suit and a woman huddled behind him.

Anton snorted. "No offense, Winger, but I'm going to have to check to make sure you're not packing a few more pistols."

The teenager Josh had seen in the parlor materialized at his side. The boy found Josh's knife and another gun, the only weapons Josh had carried.

Except, of course, for his fists. And frankly, Josh had never relied fully upon any other weapon. He could take Anton and whatever teenage army was hiding in the dark cellar, if only he could get Lexi safely out of here.

"You know me." Josh stalled while he started making mental note of his surroundings—wine racks, casks, barrels. Yet on the other side of the cellar, he could discern the outline of rolling racks and fabric bolts, the same tools of a designer's trade that Amanda Matthews kept at the loft.

"You took care of blasting one of my traitorous lieutenants this summer, remember? I figured you were probably still on my case when I saw you talking to Lexi last night at the Dance for Children."

The woman sobbing next to Anton cried louder, drawing Josh's attention back to the two figures at the back of the room. Now that Josh's eyes had fully adjusted to the lack of light, he studied the bent figure carefully, scared that Lexi had somehow injured herself in her struggle with the elder Bertrand.

Only the sobbing woman wasn't Lexi.

"Where the hell is she?" Panic and fury rose up in equal parts. He started forward, fully prepared to strangle the rich-boy scumbag if Lexi was already—
"If you hurt her—"

No threat sounded dire enough for what Josh would do to the man if he'd harmed Lex.

Before Josh could tear apart the Ivy League criminal along with his three-piece suit, Anton curled an arm around his sister's head and buried the barrel in Simone's tangled blond hair.

At the same time, the soft *click* of a safety going off registered in his consciousness from somewhere behind him. No doubt the teenager had a gun pointed at Josh's back.

"Not a chance in hell you'll shoot your own sister." Nevertheless, Josh halted his forward momentum. Simone's face had gone as white as her platinum curls.

"I spent all night celebrating my latest importing mission with a variety of designer drugs and some of the wine cellar's finest offerings. Now I'm hungover, slightly high and desperate. Do you really think I care who I kill today?"

The guy had all but admitted to his crimes, and Josh didn't feel the slightest bit of triumph. Only one concern resounded in his mind.

Josh raised his hands a little higher, needing to make sure this situation didn't get out of control. "I'm cool. I just want to know where Lexi is."

He reminded himself to breathe, to think. In over a decade of being a cop, Josh had never sweated out a moment like this. But then, nothing had ever threatened a woman he loved.

A hell of a time to realize he loved her, damn it, but maybe he had needed the knockout punch to help him figure it out.

"She got away," Anton admitted, absently stroking his sister's cheek with one hand while he held the gun to her head with another. "For all I know, she's hiding in the wine racks. Brad, I'll cover the cop. You find the girl.''

Anton hadn't hurt her.

Relief, hope washed through him.

In the background, he heard Duke pounding on the door to the wine cellar. And somewhere in his mind, he recognized the fact that Anton was getting scared, maybe even stupid.

But Josh's first order of business was scanning the cool, dry cellar for any sign of Lexi. If he was going to ensure her safety, he needed to know if she was down here.

He'd done a lousy job of protecting her up until now, but starting today, that was all going to change.

"Just a minute, pig!" Anton shouted toward the door, toward Duke on the other side of it. "I've got a cop at gunpoint in here, I don't think you want to piss me off.''

Josh shook his head. *Bad move, Anton.* He was about to warn the strung-out smuggler against bluffing the NYPD, when he saw her.

Lexi.

His eyes rested on an industrial-size bolt of orange silky fabric lying on its side in a pile with several other bolts. Only this bolt had one lone black curl springing through one end of the roll to trail down the yards of bright silk.

Smart woman.

It was all Josh could do not to smile, he was so relieved. He just hoped she knew enough to stay put and remain hidden.

Because now that he knew where Lexi hid, he could go about saving her.

And after all she'd done for him, by God, he owed her that much.

SAVE ME.

Lexi chanted the words in her head as Brad moved closer to her hiding spot, not caring if that made her the world's most desperate, needy woman. In fact, she felt pretty damn desperate and needy as she listened to her longtime friend saying he didn't care if he killed his own sister.

If Anton would shoot Simone, he surely wouldn't wince at killing Josh. The thought paralyzed her.

She'd escaped from Anton with a quick chop to the family jewels, a move she'd perfected on the dummy in self-defense class. Of course, she could also run like hell, and that had helped her lose Anton in the cellar.

But now, all she could do was hide, unless Josh could somehow save her. If Anton found her, he was going to be more than a little upset with her.

Panic twisted her insides now, but despite the icy claw of fear around her throat, she heard Josh's words filter through her cardboard cocoon.

"...forget looking for Lexi, Bertrand. She's probably halfway back to Manhattan by now."

The rifling around in the wine cellar seemed to stop.

"The door locks automatically when it's shut," Anton argued. "She couldn't have gotten out of here."

"She's probably smarter than ten of you put together, bud. I wouldn't count on it."

Lexi surprised herself by choosing that moment to smile. She was still scared, but Josh's words soothed her just a little.

Anton snorted. "Don't tell me you're a sap for the ice princess, too. You and James can sing her praises all you want. She'll always be a Jersey girl trying to pass herself off as a Manhattan socialite."

The two-faced traitor. Bad enough he was terrorizing her with a gun. Now he was going to trash her Jersey roots? Anger replaced a little more of her fear.

"Lexi's no ice princess. Maybe she just hides—" Josh paused a split second "—her feelings. She has good sense keeping her emotions out of sight in her line of work."

Out of sight.

Josh was sending her a message. Telling her to keep hidden. She could feel it in the tension of his words, the off-kilter syntax of his speech.

"Besides, Lexi's the toast of the town and she's going to single-handedly raise enough money to cure cancer. Why the hell would she need a place in the social register?"

Her heart did a back flip. Josh had spoken the words for her. *To* her. Because he knew she was listening.

"Now, why don't you let Simone go and hand over the guns. There are probably a truckload of cops on your lawn by now, and the media, too."

Anton laughed. "Lucky for me, the wine cellar has an exit in the rocks over the North Shore. I'll wave to your cop friends from my boat as Simone and I speed out of Long Island Sound.''

There was a scuffle in the wine cellar. A scrape of shoes on concrete, the sound of people moving around.

Lexi edged herself upward in her cardboard tunnel, needing to look out at what was going on. No matter what Josh had said about staying hidden, she wasn't about to let him get hurt.

Peering over the edge of her hiding place, Lexi could see Anton pushing Simone across the room, his gun tucked under her jaw. Brad kept his gun on Josh, but he, too, shifted positions to stand near a door in the floor Lexi guessed must lead to the beach and the escape boat.

What if they shot Josh in order to get away?

She had no choice but to ignore Josh's warning. Scooting to the end of the bolt, Lexi pushed herself out into the cellar again, careful to remain in the shadows of rolling racks and piles of fabric.

Tension gripped her as she kept her eyes trained on the sleek metal of the guns. She needed to be ready in case—

Josh made his move just as Anton released Simone to pry open the door in the cellar floor.

He dove for Anton's weapon, heedless of the armed and nervous teen behind him.

Brad lunged for Josh, jumping on his back like a monkey before he cracked Josh in the head with his gun.

Simone shrieked in time with Lexi's squeal. As Josh fell sideways with the kid still on top of him,

Lexi ran to the wine rack and yanked a bottle from its cradle.

Without any real plan in mind other than to distract the bad guys, Lexi smashed the bottle against the rack, shattering the glass and sending a shower of shards and merlot around the room.

''What the—?'' Anton's head swiveled toward her like a compass to due north.

In fact, for that split second, all eyes were on her in the center of the wine cellar. But for the first time, Lexi had no clue what to do, now that she had the limelight. She stood there with a broken half of a glass bottle, wine dripping down her arm and cuts on her fingers, waiting for guns to start firing.

They didn't.

Josh rose from the floor like Lazarus from the dead, a welt the size of Texas on his eye and a glower on his face unlike any she'd ever seen before.

In the space of two seconds, he raised both his arms and clotheslined the two gun-wielding smugglers, falling on top of them like an avalanche.

Two guns went flying in separate directions on the floor.

Out of Lexi's peripheral vision, she noticed Simone scurry to pick them up. But Lexi couldn't seem to take her main focus off Josh the Avenger wreaking havoc with the men who had scared the hell out of her.

Why did the man carry a gun if he had fists that fast? Right hook and down went Anton. Left hook and down went Brad.

Ding, ding, ding. End of round two.

The crooks were clearly down for the count, and Josh was the undisputed champ.

"Are you okay?" He turned to her, her warrior hero with the swollen eye, his glower fading into something that definitely resembled concern. Worry. Fear.

God, maybe even something more.

Before Lexi could pinpoint the look that made her heart palpitate, the entrance behind them filled with cops. Simone held the arched wooden door for the flood of men in blue led by Duke and Otis.

Lexi might have smiled at the tender way Otis lifted the guns out of Simone's hands, or the way the rookie cop scrounged a blanket to wrap around her shoulders. But she was too busy trying to figure out if she'd really seen something soft and warm in Josh's gray eyes a moment ago.

She squinted through the suddenly crowded room for a glimpse of Josh, but he was encircled by a wall of blue. His cop friends hauled Anton and Brad out of the cellar in handcuffs, making Lexi very grateful for those clever metal rings for the second time in her life.

Detectives were already searching the wine racks and exploring the casks and barrels for goods Anton might have smuggled.

She needed to see Josh. Wanted to touch him, make sure he was okay. But she'd lost her shoes somewhere along the way and shattered glass still covered the floor. She also felt lost, alone and utterly ignored, until a big shadow fell over her.

"Jesus, woman, are you okay?" Josh put his hands

on her shoulders, then tipped her chin up to look at him.

"I'm fine." Relief, warmth flowed through her.

Gently, he lifted her wrist and extracted the broken wine bottle from her hand. She'd forgotten she was even holding it.

"I was never so scared as when I saw you running around here when those guys were all over me. Didn't you understand I needed you to stay hidden?" He set the remains of the bottle in an empty wine cradle behind her.

"How could I, when you were in trouble?" His swollen eye reminded her how close he'd come to really getting hurt. Badly. Permanently.

"How could you not, Lex? You might know everything there is to know about fashion, but you don't know the first thing about fending off lethal criminals."

Incensed, she sent him a look that had made lesser men run for cover. "I know enough to flip you butt-backward over my shoulder, don't forget."

He swiped a hand over his jaw, maybe in a fit of impatience, maybe to hide a smile. She couldn't be quite sure.

He shook his head. "You caught me off guard."

"I caught them pretty off guard today, too."

"I'll say. You scared the hell out of me, too, when you blasted that bottle into five million pieces." His hands settled back on her arms, sliding up and down the sleeves of her jacket as if he were assuring himself she was really in one piece.

"I can cause quite a distraction when I want to."

"Lady, you distract me all the time." He cupped her chin in one hand, oblivious to the busy swarm of cop activity around them. "I probably don't want to know, but what did you think you were going to do with that broken bottle?"

She traced one finger along the scar on Josh's cheek, just below his black eye, trying really, really hard not to throw herself in his arms. "You might be able to fend off broken glass, but a lot of people wouldn't be able to."

He halted her tentative touch with the vise of his hand. "We need to talk, Lex. But not here. Not now." He scooped her off her feet and into his arms, carrying her over the shattered remains of the bottle through the cellar. "I need to find enough evidence to lock up Bertrand for a lifetime, and I can't do it with you standing there, making me want to think other things."

"Wait, Josh." She didn't need to be hauled around like a sack of potatoes, but then again, she rather liked the sensation of being tucked up against his chest.

Too bad he dumped her off with James, as her old teacher and friend was coming down to the cellar. "James will find you a cup of coffee until I finish up down here. You'll be more comfortable upstairs where you can't step on any broken glass."

With that, he pivoted and rejoined the fracas of swarming New York police detectives at the crime scene.

Lexi's eyes burned. He was worried about broken glass? The oaf obviously had no clue he'd just delivered a more painful blow than anything she'd experienced in the cellar with Anton.

He'd dismissed her from his world.

Again.

Her time as Sherlock Holmes had clearly come to an end, and Josh had little use for a limelight-seeking fashion critic. But no matter how many times she repeated "his loss" to herself, she couldn't help but think she'd been the one to lose something irreplaceable today.

16

JOSH HAD NEVER taken less pleasure from tying up a case.

The process of gathering evidence seemed interminable, but finally they'd secured a red cashmere sweater from Anton's closet that looked like it would match the fibers Lexi's dog had found at the arson scene. It was a man's sweater, not a woman's. But sure enough, the label read Valentino, just as Lexi had predicted, and there was a tear along the hem.

Smart woman.

Josh jogged up the stairs and through the Bertrand mansion, eager to find her, eager to beg her to be his.

He found the butler in the kitchen, picking up teacups and piling them in the sink.

Josh slowed his pace. "Where's Lexi?"

"Her cab just arrived. She's headed back to Manhattan." James's stern look communicated to Josh how badly he'd screwed up by depositing her in the kitchen for the past hour and a half.

Shit.

Josh ran to catch her, stealing a glimpse of the bright yellow car out the window before he sprinted through the front door.

He shouted and waved, attracting Lexi's attention,

along with that of a bevy of reporters milling around the lawn.

The media thronged him, quickly cueing in to the presence of the lead detective on a late-breaking case. They stuffed microphones in his face, flashed camera bulbs in his eyes and shouted one question on top of another.

Welcome to the circus.

His first instinct was to plow through the press ranks and make a last-ditch effort with Lexi before she cruised out of his life forever. Talking to the media had never been his forte.

Then again, he'd never really given it a shot.

A camera bulb flashed in his face, in time with the lightbulb slowing going off in his head. A plan came to him with startling clarity—a way to show Lexi he was ready for a life with her.

Public or private.

LEXI PAUSED, waiting for Josh to snarl at the crowds, disperse them with one heartfelt glower from his bruised face.

Maybe in some recess of her mind she thought it would be easier to leave if she saw him send cameras flying and reporters scurrying. She told herself that once she had that proof that they could never mesh their worlds, she'd be able to slide inside the cab.

Oddly, there didn't seem to be a stampede. In fact, the reporters now moved out in a more organized circle, giving the man in their midst a little more space.

Curious, Lexi asked the cabdriver to wait, then slammed the door shut behind her. If anyone else were in the center of that ring of news journalists, Lexi would assume the person was getting ready to give a press conference.

But this was Josh Winger, undercover man. No way would he be—

"I'd like to make a statement, if I may." Josh's voice boomed over the lawn, broadcast via someone's microphone and a makeshift sound system the press had organized collectively.

Lexi edged closer to the circle, the cold fall grass freezing her bare toes on the lawn, but she couldn't seem to walk away from Josh's unusual public appearance.

Didn't he hate to be in the spotlight?

At first, he recapped the events of the day, ending with the news that the NYPD had cracked a smuggling ring and now possessed enough evidence to put its leaders behind bars for a very long time.

His delivery was smooth, his presence commanding. In fact, she could hardly take her eyes off him, much less think of walking back toward her cab.

How could he have remained behind the scenes for so long in his work when he was clearly an articulate public speaker and the perfect poster boy for the police department? If she saw this man on TV representing the strength of the NYPD, she'd sure as hell never commit a crime.

"And I'd like to give credit to Lexi Mansfield for helping the police catch these criminals," Josh continued. "At great personal risk to herself, Ms. Mansfield helped us secure enough evidence that we believe will convict Anton Bertrand."

Lexi wasn't sure, but she thought she might be blushing. Her cheeks heated at his public praise.

Just when she thought he would sew up his comments, he turned to look directly at her, where she stood at the back of the crowd.

"Also, I'd like to announce I'm leaving undercover work after I settle the fallout from this case."

The crowd of reporters, who had been well mannered up until now, barraged him with questions, moving in on the circle of space he'd carved out for himself.

Lexi made an effort to close her mouth, which had gaped open in shock. How could Josh be anything but a cop? Especially now that he was meeting the press and taking on a bigger role. He'd be leading his own precinct in another couple of years at this rate.

The media's unanimous cry of "why?" echoed her own.

"I'm in the process of making professional plans I do not wish to reveal at this time." Still, his eyes remained on Lexi, lingering for so long that members of the press corps began to turn around to look at her, too.

"But I can say," Josh continued from his spot at center stage, "you'd better get ready to film the wildest courtship this town has ever seen. I'm out to win New York's prized fashion critic for my very own."

A ripple of *ooh*s and *aah*s moved through the crowd.

Several cameras moved from Josh toward her. Camera bulbs flashed. Shutters clicked.

And Lexi would appear in tomorrow's paper looking like a wrung-out rag and utterly dumbfounded.

Shock robbed her of speech. Fear that this was all somehow a joke kept her from sprinting through the crowd to fling herself around the man she wanted more than anything.

Luckily, Josh had turned into Mr. Microphone and deftly directed everyone's attention back to him. "I might even offer up a reward to anybody who can help me figure out how to clinch a wedding date in less than six months. That's the end of my statement, ladies and gentlemen, and I'd appreciate it if you could respect that Ms. Mansfield and I have had a long and difficult day."

Just like that, Josh had the crowd backing up, thanking him for his words and discreetly fading into the background.

She'd never seen a man more perfectly suited for life in the public eye, and she couldn't believe he might actually want to be a part of hers.

And then, he was there. "Come on." Without prelude, he tugged her along the lawn, pulling her behind a row of cedar trees and into a small wooden playhouse Simone had used as a little girl. "I can't believe you didn't find yourself a pair of shoes."

The wooden floor felt warm enough on her toes, and Lexi was thankful for the privacy the space afforded them amid the busy hubbub of the main house. Hope surged through her, tempered by wariness. She seated herself on the built-in table against one wall.

"Are you out of your mind?" She couldn't stall the question that burned in her brain as she stared out over the child's dream house with its faded pink curtains and stenciled ponies on the walls.

"For what?" He sat down on the table beside her, planting his feet on the bench next to it. "Chasing New York's sexiest journalist?"

A little thrill sizzled through her at the look he shot her way, but she couldn't afford to get distracted by *that* right now. "That blow to the head is affecting you more than you realize, Winger. You love being an undercover man. Why would you ever do anything else?"

"It's a job that has a limited shelf life, and I've made enough headlines this summer to realize my time undercover is up. I need new challenges."

"Like?"

"Like protecting you from all the trouble you get into in your line of work, for one thing. A woman like you attracts too much attention and more trouble than you can possibly handle."

This was not exactly the sort of proposal she'd hoped for. She'd refused to get her hopes up, and for good reason.

"Now that Anton is going to jail," she countered, "I don't have a thing to worry about. He was the one who set my apartment on fire, wasn't he?"

Josh nodded, fingering one of her curls where it lay on the shoulder of her jacket. "He wanted you to stop writing negative things about Simone's designs, because if her business went under, so did his smuggling operation. He was using her business as a cover for importing his stuff." Josh smoothed the stray curl into the rest of her hair. "Little did he know, he didn't stand a chance of reining in your opinions."

She shrugged, unrepentant. "I have this great need to be heard."

"And I have this great need to make sure you're safe while you're speaking your mind. So if it's all the same to you, while I figure out what area I want to concentrate on at the precinct, I'm also going to head up security for Lexi Mansfield."

Security? What about the marriage thing he'd mentioned in front of ten different television cameras? Didn't the man have any clue she wanted to hear about that?

"Protecting me from the paparazzi and your stray weirdos is hardly challenge enough for a man of your skills." He would be bored with her inside of two weeks. Maybe five, because she could keep him pretty entertained with just great sex for a while.

He laughed, a gesture that scrunched up the swollen skin around his eye and looked pretty painful to Lexi.

"Life with you could never be boring, Lexi. You're like a one-woman show. And when *you* get bored of *me,* then I'll move into police intervention work for at-risk teens like Brad and other kids who get roped into working for crooks just because they're poor and desperate."

The idea of Josh saving would-be thugs from themselves just about stole her heart. Too bad she was already losing him to another, more worthy occupation, and she hadn't even had the benefit of his bodyguard skills yet. "You'd be great at that. You're like a walking advertisement for how to be a tough guy and honorable at the same time.''

"I know who to go to if I need help getting a charitable endeavor off the ground, right?'' He looked ready to jump up and take on the world, in spite of the bruised outline of a gun against his temple.

She smiled even as she shed a few tears inside. How could he save her, say he wanted to marry her, and then make plans to leave her all in the same day? "I've never met a cause I didn't like.''

"What about me?'' He swiveled to face her on the small wooden table, taking her hands in his own.

"What about you?''

"Make me your cause, Lex, and rescue me from a life of anonymity.''

She sidled closer, wondering if they were getting back around to the marriage thing. "If that's your idea of a proposal, Josh Winger, I can tell you you've got your work cut out for you.''

His gaze narrowed, darkened, focused on her lips. "My idea of a proposal involves two rings, two hand-cuffs and a lifetime of sexy bondage.''

Her pulse kicked into overdrive. Hope reared its irrepressible head and put a lump in her throat. "Tiger, those words turn my head and rev my body, but they won't ever wrest a 'yes' from my lips.''

"No?'' He kissed her cheek, her jaw, the side of her lips. "Then, how's this?'' He shifted her off her seat and onto his lap. When he had her cradled on his thighs, he found her left hand and circled her third finger with his hand.

"I love you, Lexi Mansfield, and I want to make

you my wife, my woman and my partner. I can't promise you anything fancy or that I'll be the most suave guy at your fund-raisers, but I can promise I'll always be there, by your side. And I promise I will always listen to you, and never, ever ignore you.''

The shell around her carefully guarded heart cracked and broke. She'd never felt so warm and gushy inside, so full of love she thought she'd explode with it.

This gorgeous, sexy, tough-as-steel guy wanted her.

''You love me?'' She'd never been given such a gift.

''You and your blue toenails walk on water as far as I'm concerned.''

Lexi flung herself around him, squeezed him, kissed the uninjured side of his face. ''I love you, Josh. Adore you. And if you think I'm waiting six months to claim you as my man, you're insane.''

He probably had to expend considerable effort to peel her off him, because she didn't ever want to let him go.

''You mean it?''

''*Gawd*, yes. I've loved you since that time we wrestled around on the carpet with all the lights on, but I was too scared to admit it, even to myself. Are you sure you're not going to mind a life in the spotlight?''

Even now, the sounds of relentless reporters creeping in the bushes outside the playhouse reached their ears.

''Not as long as I can spirit you away to the shadows every now and then, too.'' He slid his hand up her thigh to the hem of her skirt, careful to keep her covered from the camera that suddenly appeared in a window across the playhouse from them.

Would he tell them to get lost? Break the camera for intruding?

Lexi feigned obliviousness, waiting to gauge his reaction. This was the downside to public life, but she wasn't about to give it up.

''What about your work?'' she prodded, still not quite believing Josh was ready to leave his under-cover days behind. ''Will you still get to work with Duke, or will he be losing his partner if you do some-thing else on the force?'' She straightened his collar, smoothed his shirt where it had been ripped down the front.

''Duke's gaining a pseudo sister-in-law and now he doesn't have to break my legs for messing around with you, so don't you worry about him. Besides, if I can't always be out in the field, Duke can take Otis around and show him the ropes.'' His hand molded over her thigh, down her knee and back up again, staunchly ignoring the intrusion of the camera.

Lexi shivered in response to his touch, his cool demeanor in light of their not-so-private moment. Life with this man was going to be so delicious. ''Snow-ball is going to be so happy when I bring you home with me on a full-time basis.''

''Did I mention I'm thinking about getting a rott-weiler?''

''Did I mention the poodles of the world have a way of bringing rottweilers to their knees?'' She splayed her hand over his chest, stroking her finger-nails down the white cotton.

"No. But you can tell me all about it when I come over to the loft with the two rings and a pair of hand-cuffs tonight." His hand inched a little higher under her skirt.

"Is that right? If you play your cards right, maybe I'll use those handcuffs to bring *you* to your knees."

Josh drew her closer, flexed his arm against the small of her back to press them together, and kissed her in full view of the camera lens. "Honey, I think you already have."

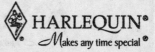